Elizabe

Good Society

Or, contrasts of character. In three volumes. Vol. 3

SALZWASSER
VERLAG

Elizabeth Caroline Grey

Good Society

Or, contrasts of character. In three volumes. Vol. 3

Reprint of the original, first published in 1863.

1st Edition 2022 | ISBN: 978-3-37500-700-3

Verlag (Publisher): Salzwasser Verlag GmbH, Zeilweg 44, 60439 Frankfurt, Deutschland
Vertretungsberechtigt (Authorized to represent): E. Roepke, Zeilweg 44, 60439 Frankfurt, Deutschland
Druck (Print): Books on Demand GmbH, In de Tarpen 42, 22848 Norderstedt, Deutschland

GOOD SOCIETY.

VOL. III.

GOOD SOCIETY;

OR,

CONTRASTS OF CHARACTER.

BY

MRS. GREY,

AUTHOR OF

"THE GAMBLER'S WIFE,"
"PASSAGES IN THE LIFE OF A FAST YOUNG LADY,"
&c.

IN THREE VOLUMES.

VOL. III.

LONDON:

1863.

GOOD SOCIETY;

OR,

CONTRASTS OF CHARACTER.

CHAPTER I.

UNEXPECTED ADVANTAGES.

A FEW days after the dinner at Mount-Trevor Court, Mr. Drelincourt was sitting by himself at a library table, in an apartment usually designated in the establishment "the study;" though what was studied there no one seemed able to state with sufficient decision to satisfy the rest. There were books enough round the room, every one agreed, to teach everything that could be worth knowing.

In truth, it was a well selected collection in handsome bindings, placed in the most perfect order—folios, quartos, octavos, duodecimos, each by themselves; and history, biography, science, poetry, classics, religion, and art, in separate divisions. The books of reference were on one shelf, and the more light reading within easy access. Conspicuous among the most used volumes was a set of Shakspeare and another of the "Spectator."

No one could take it for the library of an idler—the useful books formed too large a portion of the collection. Indeed, it was easy to see that it was the library of a man of business.

The circular table contained a massive silver inkstand, a case of stationery, blotting-pad, and a variety of fancy articles usually found in such places in the houses of persons of wealth. There were also several rolls of paper and parchment, and piles of folded and endorsed papers—something in the style of the office of a land surveyor in extensive practice.

Mr. Drelincourt was not, however, looking either at his books or at his papers. He seemed absorbed in a calculation which he was making on a sheet of foolscap, looking occasionally at a small vellum-bound volume with a lock on it to denote the privacy required for its contents.

It was evident that he was not dissatisfied, for he went over his figures with quite as pleasant a countenance as he exhibited when he sipped his port-wine. And when he had worked his sum, he looked as thoroughly happy as any persevering school-boy who has triumphed over the "vexation" of his first numerical achievement in compound multiplication.

The little volume close to his left hand was his cash-book, and the numerous figures upon the sheet of foolscap formed a schedule of expenses contemplated for improvements on "The Hall Estate." This included with the expenses of planting, draining the land, the erection of a model farm, with every description of steam apparatus that had been found useful, the rebuilding the church, schools, and parsonage, made a sum total that might have alarmed some capitalists. The amount, however, large as it was, did not make up the entire contemplated expenditure; another source of expense had recently been suggested to him, that would demand a much larger outlay, and this he had duly considered and decided upon incurring.

As he was locking the little volume, the butler entered, and announced "Professor Grauwacke."

"Ah! you are punctual to your time," observed Mr. Drelincourt, as he glanced at the time-piece over the fire-place.

"O yes! inteed it is best to be bunctual," replied the Doctor, looking intensely amiable through his coloured glasses, "barticular when I call on gentlemens whose time is brecious, mine goot sir."

"Take a seat, Professor, and let us discuss this matter simply as a business transaction. I have looked into it carefully, and am quite disposed to take it up,—that is, of course, if there can be no question of its *bonâ fide* character. A speculation is one thing, Doctor; but if what you tell me is a demonstrable fact, the thing is better than a speculation."

Professor Grauwacke rubbed his hands together, and his face was lit up with a sense of triumph that rendered its expression exceedingly cheerful. He looked elevated to the seventh heaven of scientific ecstacy.

"I will bledge my knowledge of the geological science," he said, impressively, "that the survey I have had the great honour to make of your fine, noble, highly to be appreciated property, is all truth,—everyting, from beginning to end."

"You are sure, Professor, that there is lead in sufficient quantity to pay a fair profit on the capital that must be invested in working it?"

"I have most bleasure to assure you that the magnesian limestone is full of galena, containing a large per-centage of silver. There cannot be a doubt that it will prove of a prodigiously to be estimated value, mine goot sir. There are at the next town two English gentlemens who have had much renown among geologists here in England. You shall send for them, or for any other combetent persons; and you shall have the specimens analyzed by any practical chemist of goot repute; and they shall say that I am quite right in every barticular of my report."

Professor Grauwacke again rubbed his hands, and his eyes again flashed with triumph. He saw before him a prospect of almost unlimited thalers; for whether he should be rewarded by a per-centage on the yield, or should receive a bonus for its discovery, he was quite certain that his recompense would prove a liberal one.

Mr. Drelincourt was too much a man of business to make any advance on the representations of a stranger of whom he knew very little. He therefore gave his visitor to understand that he would be paid handsomely for the information he had given, but that its accuracy must in the first place be tested in the most reliable manner possible.

The Professor only rubbed his hands more energetically, and looked exultant, at this intimation. He was quite content—so thoroughly so that he seemed to have ignored the great German question in which he had hitherto felt so absorbing an interest. The fact was, he anticipated a material advantage, more lasting in its benefit than a pecuniary reward. He looked for constant occupation as superintendent of the new lead mines, as well as a great scientific reputation in the country of which he had become a denizen.

So after some details had been gone into

respecting the stratification of the neighbourhood, the Professor took leave of his patron, with a promise from the latter of a communication as soon as the question had been decided by the persons to whom he intended to refer it.

Mr. Drelincourt was again left alone. Once more he cast his eyes over the figures he had made on the foolscap, and had just satisfied himself of their correctness, when the door was opened by the butler. Sonorously he announced the names of Sir Pouncefort Pouncefort, the Hon. Major-General Toplofty and Admiral Lord Bluffington.

The master of the Hall rose promptly to receive such distinguished guests, not a little puzzled to account for their joint visit. They entered, each hat in hand, looking stiff and consequential, yet with an air of very considerable cordiality. They shook hands with their host, who had seats placed for them, and expressed his gratification at seeing them at the Hall; in short, was as courteous as his exceeding good nature would permit him to be. Yet he could not satisfy himself as to what brought them there.

"Getting up a subscription," I dare say, he thought to himself.

"Now I like to be frank, Mr. Drelincourt," began Sir Pouncefort Pouncefort abruptly; "it's the characteristic of an Englishman, and distinguishes us from foreigners, who always make it a point to mislead every one who trusts in their professions. The palladium of civil and religious liberty, which is the birthright of an Englishman——"

"Hear! hear!" cried the Admiral and the Major-General, vehemently.

"Ought to make him frank in all his social relations, particularly when he has something exceedingly important to communicate."

"Hear! hear!" shouted the county magnates, looking Mr. Drelincourt full in the face.

"What on earth can these people be driving at?" Mr. Drelincourt asked himself, and, of course, asked in vain.

"A communication to make," said the orator, with marked emphasis, and looking at his host as if going to take his portrait, "of the very greatest importance, to a friend in whom he is about to place the greatest possible confidence."

"Hear! hear!" vociferated the others, apparently determined to stare their friend out of countenance.

"Gentlemen, I feel exceedingly flattered," commenced the master of the Hall; but what he was flattered about it would have puzzled him to state.

"We have the highest opinion of you, Mr. Drelincourt!" cried the Major-General, with extreme decision of manner.

"The county esteem your talents and honour your principles, sir!" added Admiral Lord Bluffington, with something very like fierceness in his look.

"My lord, gentlemen, believe me I am very proud of your good opinion; but I am afraid that I have resided too short a time in the county to deserve the appreciation your lordship has so kindly expressed."

"As a great man—unfortunately now no more—has said, Mr. Drelincourt," recommenced the orator of the party, "there is no mistake—there can be no mistake."

"Hear! hear!" again shouted the naval and military contingent.

Their host looked from one to the other, as if asking for explanation.

"It is quite out of the question that there should be any mistake about Mr. Drelincourt. Indeed, I think I may be permitted to say that, as far as regards myself, and as far as regards the other honourable members of this deputation, a mistake is impossible."

Again the "Hear, hear!" of his two companions rose loud and sharp, and once more the greatly-puzzled host turned an inquiring glance in their direction. But no solution of the mystery was perceptible in their hard inscrutable features, as he looked from one to the other. The purple-visaged baronet, the white-moustached General, and the fiery-faced Admiral with the weak eyes, continued to gaze on him as solemn as owls.

"You would really oblige me very much," said the retired merchant, "if you would kindly inform me of the purpose of your visit."

"Viscount Cassington has been appointed *attaché* to the Embassy at Constantinople," announced the venerable baronet.

The county magnates simultaneously drew

their chairs nearer to their host, and simultaneously stared at him harder than ever.

"I am glad to hear it," he quietly replied, "both for his lordship's sake and for the sake of his right honourable parents, to whom I have no doubt it will be a source of great gratification, as the first step in a career of distinction worthy of the social position of his family. I beg to express to you my sincere thanks for the trouble you have taken in coming to the Hall, to acquaint me with this interesting fact; but pardon me if I say I cannot see what particular interest I can have in the intelligence."

The baronet looked significantly at his friends, and his friends at him; and then they all looked significantly at Mr. Drelincourt.

"Lord Cassington's appointment," said the Baronet, solemnly, "makes a vacancy in the county representation."

Again simultaneously they all drew their chairs nearer to their host, and gazed at him as hard as they could.

"Well, Sir Pouncefort?"

"Our business here is to offer the vacant

seat to our respected friend, John Drelincourt, Esq., of the Hall!"

"Hear! hear!" shouted the Major-General and the Admiral, with stentorian voices.

There was a pause. The retired merchant was taken so much by surprise by the proposal that he could scarcely realize it.

"Do you mean to say, my dear Sir Pouncefort?" he inquired, in an agitated manner, "that you and your influential friends, the Honourable Major-General Toplofty, and Admiral Lord Bluffington, have done me the unspeakable honour to consider me as a proper representative for the county?"

"We do!" chorused the deputation, determinedly.

"It is impossible for me to express my gratitude, Sir Pouncefort; you have laid me under a heavy load of obligation, my Lord. General, I can never forget this extraordinary service."

"Will you allow yourself to be put in nomination, my dear Drelincourt?" inquired the venerable Baronet, after their candidate had been shaken warmly by the hand, by each of his supporters.

"I place myself entirely in your hands," he answered cheerfully. "No one can know better than yourself, Sir Pouncefort, what is most proper under the circumstances."

"There can't be a doubt of that," cried Admiral Lord Bluffington, winking one of his ferrety eyes under the green shade.

"O, he's a first-rate campaigner!" added the Honourable Major-General Toplofty. "And the county knows it."

"And the county knows it," echoed his naval colleague.

The six weeks' county member endeavoured to bear this estimation modestly; but the sense of pride that suffused his countenance with a more purple tint, betrayed his intense satisfaction.

"I hope I do my duty by the county," he replied. "I hope I do my duty. But it is only justice to add that we all do our duty, and I am quite certain that we cannot do it more completely than by advancing the election of our excellent friend here."

"Of course, of course!" cried the Admiral.

"I am at his service, as soon as he gives the word of command," added the Major-General.

"A thousand thanks!" exclaimed their host. "But might I venture to ask if the Marquis is aware of your kind interposition in my favour?"

"We have come direct from Mount-Trevor Court," replied the venerable Baronet. "The fact is, the county are well aware of the claims the Marquis has on their support; but I think I may be permitted to say in confidence, that the county requires the services of an energetic, able, solid man of business, with high oratorical qualifications, combined with advanced political views."

"Ah, that's it!" said the Admiral, exultingly.

"We know the sort of man the county wants, my dear Drelincourt," cried the Major-General, much in the same tone.

The retired merchant bowed, and looked the gratification he felt. To say no more than the truth, he had never been more gratified in his life.

"Lord Cassington, between ourselves," continued the orator, "has proved himself too much a man of pleasure, to be entrusted with the interests of so important a constituency."

"But then, there is his brother, Lord Lionel," said Mr. Drelincourt. "Really a very superior young man."

"Yes, my dear Drelincourt, he is by far the better man for a member of parliament, of the two. But the Marquis has no intention of putting him forward in a political career at present. My impression is that he waits for the general election, though it is not at all unlikely that his lordship may expect another diplomatic post from his friend the Foreign Secretary. All I can say with certainty is, that on consulting his lordship upon the vacancy occasioned by the Viscount accepting his foreign appointment, the Marquis said he had no idea of starting his second son, and in a very friendly way suggested yourself."

Mr. Drelincourt expressed his acknowledgments warmly.

Lord Mount-Trevor was not quite so disinterested in making this suggestion, as the object of it was willing to believe. No one knew better what he was about than that patrician Paterfamilias. He was the last man in the peerage likely to neglect the interests of his family, though it must be confessed that some of his actions, to common-place observers, seemed to be as little conducive to their real advantage as to his own dignity.

Mr. Drelincourt elevated, as he unquestionably was, at the brilliant prospect thus unexpectedly opening before him, did not forget his business habits. He began to question the deputation as to his proceedings as a candidate, and soon ascertained that the transaction was not likely to be so easy as it looked at first. A contest was more than probable, and if it took place would inevitably be a sharp one. There were two political parties in the county, and the other had long been attending to the registration, with the object of contesting the representation on the first favourable opportunity.

The Marquis Mount-Trevor was well aware of this; moreover, was well aware that his balance-sheet at Coutts's would not suffice for the expenses of a borough contest, much less for that of a county. His lordship therefore backed out of the affair in the graceful pleasant way in which he usually backed out of anything that promised awkward consequences, and generously proposed that his neighbour's purse should supply the means of carrying on the contest. The proposition was made with an *arriére pensée*, which afforded the Marquis considerable consolation. He did not consider that he should lose by it in any way.

The candidate pressed his questions till he had ascertained the maximum expense the contest would produce. This would be thought a serious responsibility to most country gentlemen, but the late head of the great Bristol firm treated it as a bagatelle,—not a little to the surprise, and very greatly to the gratification, of his zealous supporters; who, to say no more than the truth, had felt considerable anxiety on this point, as they were without a candidate in reserve, in a pecuniary sense, equal to the emergency, had their new friend declined so heavy an expenditure.

"I told you there could be no mistake!" exclaimed the venerable Baronet, now completely at his ease. "Rest assured that we shall have the right man in the right place this time."

"We knew it was all right," cried the Admiral, apparently overflowing with political enthusiasm. "I never was more sure of anything in my life!"

Lord Bluffington was as positive as he was determined, but was not the more to be depended upon on that account.

"Sure!" repeated the Major-General, with a laugh that showed how much he ridiculed the idea of opposition. "It was impossible to be more certain!"

Notwithstanding that officer's assumed confidence, he knew perfectly well, the Admiral knew perfoctly well, and the Baronet knew perfectly well, that the election was by no means so certain a thing as they affected to believe it was. The duty of the county magnates was clearly to induce the rich man to supply funds sufficient to defeat the opposition party should they bring forward another man, and whatever they could say in the way of encouragement to their candidate was, of course, no more than they ought to do.

Mr. Drelincourt, however, was not deceived. He contrived to obtain a tolerably correct knowledge of the resources of his anticipated opponents, and was satisfied that his chance of election was a fair one. A good deal he knew on such occasions depended on individual energy and enterprise, as well as on the skilful arrangement of the machinery usually employed in such contests; and he astonished his zealous supporters by the much greater zeal he displayed in at once organizing a plan for the general canvass, in case his nomination should be opposed.

The conference lasted so long that the deputation were invited to luncheon, where they sat some time longer, not forgetting to drink success to their host, with as much noisy demonstration as if they had been a dozen instead of three. Subsequently they were taken to see the improvements which were metamorphosing the estate, with all the graces of landscape gardening. With much that was in progress they appeared to be astonished. In truth, they could not see the utility of distorting the surface of what was always considered a pleasant park, with terraces, slopes, mounds, sunk gardens, raised lakes, ferneries, fountains, a winding river, and plantations and ornamental grounds in apparently endless variety. But they praised everything, and more, were reconciled to everything, in consequence of the evidence it afforded of their friend's immense fortune.

CHAPTER II.

ROMANCE AND REALITY.

VISCOUNT CASSINGTON was not sorry to drop the M.P. that had for the last two or three years been an affix to his title. He had lately considered it rather a bore. Speech-making was not his lordship's *forte*—it would be difficult to say what was; for although he prided himself on making a betting-book, and on his knowledge of horse-flesh, he had never attended Tattersall's on a settling-day without finding that he had more to pay than to receive; and though he was up to every dodge of the stable, somehow or other he was constantly being taken in by the horse he backed.

Then he did not like parliamentary labour. His presence at debates, his attendance on committees, his waiting for divisions, he pronounced awfully slow work. Unless the discussion was enlivened by Lord Palmerston walking into some snob of a Manchester man, or by some Irish fellow abusing the Government like old boots, he never saw the most remote prospect of amusement in going to the House. The whipper-in, however, was inexorable, and the Speaker was always civil to him, so he did his best as a member.

Nevertheless, his visits to the House interfered very much with other visits which were more to his taste—particularly to the *bijou* of a house in the bye-street in Belgravia, where he was in the habit of passing his time with even less credit than his lordship gained by his slack attendance in Parliament. Though he was conscious that the fair driver of the pretty pony-carriage had lost much of her fashion, as well as a large proportion of the attractiveness she possessed when he first made her acquaintance, owing to certain grievous habits she had somehow or other contracted, the young Viscount continued to make long calls at her residence; indeed, it had been asserted that he seemed as much at home there as if he paid the rent.

The Marquis Mount-Trevor was a man of the world, as well as the father of a family. He knew a good deal of what was going on in society, and the state of affairs at the *bijou* of a furnished house in the bye-street in Belgravia, came to his knowledge as a matter of course. As a patrician Paterfamilias he did not approve of it.

Its once attractive tenant was rapidly becoming discreditable. She had ceased to be "the cynosure of neighbouring eyes" in the Hyde Park drive. The pretty turn-out had been sold to a lucky gold-digger's widow—fresh from Australia with a prodigious nugget, and a broad face, freckled and pock-marked beyond toleration.

It was plainly his duty as a father to prevent his heir disgracing himself and his family. So he exerted himself in a certain direction, and the result was that the gay young Viscount was expatriated as a certain

English admiral was shot, "*pour encourager les autres,*" according to a well-known French report of the transaction.

Lord Cassington had not the slightest objection to go to Constantinople. Certain would-be wits in his club asserted that his lordship was safe to go farther and fare worse, as he was going to Jericho as fast as he could. He had heard of harems and sultanas, of tender Circassian slaves and fascinating *houris,* of sherbet and kabobs, and of coffee and chibouques—rather a nice combination, he thought. At any rate, it would be a change from the dull task-work of the House of Commons.

But then there was the tenant of the *bijou* of a furnished house. He shrugged his aristocratic shoulders. He was getting tired of her violence. She indulged in strong expressions, which he began to think decidedly low. He was aware, too, that she not unfrequently indulged in something equally strong, which placed her, in his opinion, still lower in the social scale.

These failings were the result of her wretched youth, as she had more than once feelingly described it to him. Consequently, the good-natured Viscount was quite willing to make allowances, but could not conceal from himself that his good nature and his patience, too, were terribly abused, and that it would be as well for him to get to the Turkish capital as soon as he could.

Not that he had a very clear idea of the official duties he should there have to fulfil. He doubted whether diplomacy was more in his line than politics. In truth, his lordship had not a very exact conception of what his line was. He was not quite certain that he had a line—he could not say positively that he ever had one.

He was partial to hunting, racing, yachting, and smoking, much like other fellows, and did not mind a little exertion in the way of a ball, or of private theatricals when any pretty women were in the way, who seemed worth looking after, but he was afraid that it wouldn't suit his book to devote himself entirely either to sport or to lady-killing. Sporting was rather a bore sometimes, and to be eternally running after women was a dreadful bore.

He did not anticipate much of either of these pursuits at Constantinople. If anything of the kind should offer, it would be under such circumstances of novelty as would render it worth following. As for the performance of his duties at the Embassy he knew nothing about them—that was a special recommendation. And if they were not in his line, there would of course be no difficulty in getting some fellow to do them for him. Then if he were extra civil to the Ambassador's wife, of course it would make all square.

"But how about leaving Pussy?"

The idea of quitting his sister seemed the one real difficulty of the situation. Lord Cassington had from his youth derived all his blameless pleasures from Lady Augusta. Her strange ways and eccentric tastes had been his chief entertainment, and the warm-hearted impulsive child had so thoroughly adopted whatever she thought he liked, that he could not help regarding her as a sort of second self.

His mind was troubled about leaving her. He could not see his way at all comfortably through this contingency. In short the vivacity and originality of his favourite had so long been his amusement, that she seemed necessary to his existence.

He was aware too that the poor thing would be terribly bored by his absence, that that American spitfire would lead her an intolerable life when her old playmate was no longer at hand to laugh with her at her persecutions. Lionel would be away, and Clarence would be away, there would absolutely be no one near her, to whom the poor thing could fly, when anxious to escape from that horrid governess.

What in the world was there to be done? It was not to be thought of his taking her with him, and quite as intolerable seemed the idea of leaving her behind! He was awfully perplexed, the thing was the greatest bore he had ever known.

This train of ideas passed through the mind of Viscount Cassington, when he had sought his comfortable pillow, after enjoying a tolerable amount of amusement in the way of hunting and flirting; the day having been devoted to one, the night to the other, for the subscription pack had met in the forenoon at Sir Charles Forrester's, and the young ladies of the neighbourhood had assembled in the evening at Mount-Trevor Court.

He lay under his handsome Arabian canopy the bed clothes covered with an Eider-down quilted silk coverlet, his gold mounted dressing case open on the table, everything placed by his careful valet ready for use, and his dressing-gown and slippers on the chair within reach. He looked very like a Narcissus desirous of the favours of Morpheus, surrounded by every modern aid that luxury had suggested in the way of obtaining them. But his thoughts were in too disturbed a state to make this easy.

After a while, however, his speculations and troubles began to mingle confusedly, and at last he became conscious of a singular change of scene in which minarets and alcoves of alabaster, were grouped pleasantly with parterres of roses and fountains of perfumed water. Lutes were being played upon very sweetly by young ladies with very black eyes, and very wide trousers; and on a couch of ivory and gold a magnificent woman in a superb costume was being fanned by a black slave wearing a spangled turban, a cashmere shawl round an embroidered tunic, sky-blue trousers, and yellow slippers turned up at the toes. Suddenly the magnificent lady clapped her hands, dancing girls rushed in in very delicate drapery, and moved about as gracefully as any *corps de ballet* he had ever beheld. In truth, it was but a reminiscence of what he had witnessed scores of times on opera nights.

All at once, and with incomprehensible inconsistency, he heard the magnificent lady, who of course was a Sultana, cry out sharply—

"Cass! Cass! you must awake instantly. There are thieves in the house!"

The disturbed dreamer sat up. The moonlight streaming in at the window disclosed to his startled view as soon as he became conscious of external objects, a slight figure clothed in white, except a shawl apparently flung hurriedly over her shoulders. She was bending over him.

"Hush! are you awake!"

"Yes! What in the name of heaven and earth are you doing here?"

"I could not sleep Cass," the voice replied very softly but hurriedly, "because I heard that you were going away for a long time. So I went and sat at the window and watched the stars. Suddenly my attention was directed to the figures of three strange men stealing across the lawn. I could see them by the moonlight approaching the house, till I lost sight of them near the pantry. I opened the window cautiously and listened—then distinctly heard glass breaking. I thought it best to come and wake you, Cass, as quickly as I could."

"You've done quite right. But now go into my dressing room, I will be with you in a moment."

Lady Augusta passed through a door into an adjoining chamber, in which there was less light than in the one she had left. But she did not appear to be frightened. Presently she was joined by her brother in a pair of loose trousers and slippers. He opened the shutters noiselessly, and let in sufficient light to enable him to discern objects. He then opened a mahogany case, and took out a revolver, which he carefully examined. His sister watched him anxiously, but without betraying any alarm, as he satisfied himself that it was ready for immediate use.

"You will let me go with you, Cass?" she whispered, pleadingly.

"I think you would be safer here, Pussy."

"Do let me go with you, I'm not at all frightened!"

"I must go and wake Clarence, who's in the further room in the corridor. We will then come back for you."

"No, no! dear Cass! I could not bear to be left alone."

Her brother endeavoured to persuade her to remain locked up in the dressing-room, but she became very excited; valuable time too, as he was aware, was passing away, so he gave up the attempt, and bidding her keep close to him, preceded her out of the room; resolved, however, to place her in a position of security, before he ventured into that part of the house where the burglars had attempted to force an entrance.

They quickly reached Lord Clarence's

room, whom they found awake; a whispered summons from the partly opened door, was sufficient to bring him half clad, and only armed with a life-preserver, to their side. A brief colloquy between the brothers, produced another attempt to induce Lady Augusta to remain in safety; but she would not hear of it. Not to be detained while arguing the propriety of such an arrangement, they determined to proceed to the basement where the steward slept, in whose room they knew fire-arms were always kept loaded.

They went noiselessly along the carpeted floor, feeling their way as well as they could, for it was pitch dark, Lady Augusta keeping as close as possible to her elder brother. No one spoke, and not the slightest sound was to be heard. As soon as the young lady got to the bottom of the stairs, she turned to go through the door that opened on to a long passage that led to the offices, and proceeded on. Presently she put out her hand to satisfy herself that Lord Cassington was near her, but she no longer felt his arm—she stopped suddenly.

"Cass!" she cried, in an agonizing whisper.

But there was no answer. She felt certain that she had not followed her brother, but had taken a wrong turning. Where she was she could not tell. Still, though anxious and excited, she would not give way to fear. She felt about very carefully and advanced cautiously till she came to the wall. She felt a chair. She knew that she must be in a room.

She sat down quietly for a minute or two, as if to consider her position. Her young heart began to beat more rapidly as she distinctly heard a footstep not very far from her. She listened with painful attention, for she was certain that some one was in the apartment. She could hear his breathing. She could also hear a muttered execration as he stumbled over something that had impeded his progress. It was not either of her brothers. It must be one of the burglars.

She rose noiselessly to her feet, and was immediately aware of a sharp detonation and a sudden flash. It was a match being lit, and she saw by the lurid glare it first produced, the figure of a bulky man in a shabby suit of coarse garments, his face half covered with black crape.

The fellow glared suspiciously about while he lit a candle. Suddenly he started with an oath, when the light fell upon the white garment and face almost as pale, of a young girl watching him from the other side of the chamber.

He checked his first impulse to blow out the candle and make an attempt to escape the way he had advanced. As soon as he became satisfied that he had only a frightened girl to deal with he gained courage.

"Glad to see you, miss," said the fellow, in a husky tone, but with an attempt to be humorous. "Hopes I ain't disturbed your repose. You haven't no call to be alarmed, miss, 'cos nobody won't do you no 'arm, as sees your beautiful young face—the werry image of a girl as I had, which was just about your hage when I lost her."

Lady Augusta gave a nervous glance towards the door, as she wrapt her shawl more tightly round her. But the door was too close to the man to give her the slightest chance of escaping by it, though it was wide open, having been left so all night. The ruffian noticed the glance, and readily divined its meaning. He moved a little nearer to her, as if to cut off her flight in that direction.

"You see, miss," he now began, in a whining tone, "I'm a poor fellow as is hard up—a respectable tradesman once, miss, as kept his own wehicle; but I've been preciously ill-used. Heverybody was hard upon me, and I was sold up. I never did no good arter that, though I tried to turn a 'onest penny when I could. Then I got desprate, and went from bad to worse, miss. Sometimes I was on the tramp, and lived dreadful bad, suffering all sorts of ardships as would make your feminine eart bleed at every pore. Think of a respectable tradesman, miss, having tried everything a'most, obliged to take to cracking cribs to keep hisself and family from starving."

Lady Augusta never took her eyes for a moment off the man, but perceptibly shivered when she found that he was gradually, almost imperceptibly, approaching the place where she stood.

"Now I won't do you no arm whatsomedever," he continued, endeavouring to absorb her attention by his narrative. "You've far too good a eart, miss, to stand in a poor fellow's light, who only wants what can werry well be spared. So, if you can tell me where the plate-chest is put, I'll let you go free this minute. None o' my pals shall touch a air o' your pretty ead, miss; or, I'll let daylight into 'em with this here sharp-cutting blade, miss."

Lady Augusta set her teeth firmly against each other, and strove to overcome a sense of sickness, as the ruffian suddenly produced a murderous-looking knife, which he drew back with a sweeping movement, as though intent on cutting a throat.

"It's no use, gal, standing shilly-shally!" he now cried in a rude tone. "I don't see why I should be particlar wi' you. I'm a desprate man, and if I don't have plunder I'll have blood; so, let's have no more o' this here umbugging nonsense. *D'ye hear?*"

He sprung at and seized her by the throat. At the same moment there was a sudden flash before his eyes, and a loud report seemed to fill the air with noise and smoke. He staggered back with an oath, for the pale, apparently frightened girl had discharged a pistol at his face.

She had seen a small one in the case, with the revolver, and, unnoticed by her brother, had seized it and concealed it under her shawl. It was one of a well-known pair they had been in the habit of firing together at a mark.

Lady Augusta did not at first move from the spot where she had stood when the fellow seized her. With the discharged pistol in her hand, her eyes followed him as he fell back a pace or two; she saw him drop the murderous knife; finally she saw him clutch at the air, and then fall heavily on his back. She was again in darkness.

She heard her brother's voice in a scuffle that was going on in the offices, and, rushing forward, passed through the open door into the passage. Seeing lights in the distance, she was quickly in the middle of a group of domestics, whom the startling noise had brought from their sleeping chambers.

She urged them to hasten to the assistance of her brothers; but when they arrived at the scene of the struggle it was over. The butler, a powerful man, with Lord Cassington and Lord Clarence, all well armed, had come upon two men by surprise, as they were breaking open the plate-chest, and, after a short scuffle, had overpowered them.

On taking the crape from their faces, which was not done till after the police had arrived, they were recognized as desperate burglars, who had broken into several mansions in the county. The one who had been shot, as the reader has already anticipated, was the dog-fancier and stealer, twice introduced into this story; the other were his associates of "The Fighting Cocks"—Jem Chaffers, the ex-wax-flower hawker, and Bill Smith, the universal swindler, who, as Count Gullewski, so shamefully cheated those amiable ladies, Mrs. and Miss Bootles. In consequence of good behaviour while in prison, the latter had received a ticket-of-leave only a week before his capture.

"Just like my luck!" observed the unfortunate Bill Smith, *alias* Perkins, *alias* Johnson, *alias* "the downey one," alias the Hon. Captain Fitz-Howard, *alias* Count Theodore Gullewski. "As sure as ever I'm beginning to do a respectable stroke of business, comes these cursed Bobbies and spoils my little game!"

The policemen grinned as they secured the handcuffs on the culprits.

"I'm afraid as we're raything in the way of the likes o' you now and then," observed the sergeant. "But in this case I think I can give you the consolation that we're not likely to interfere with your game, little or big, for some considerable time."

"Gentlemen and ladies," he said, solemnly addressing the hurriedly-dressed spectators, some of whom had no stockings, some no shoes, some no coats, while others were not half dressed. "As this is my last appearance afore such a respectable and enlightened audience, permit me to announce that this sensation drama ain't to be repeated at no price."

"Here's a mollonchollу change of circumstarnces," cried the old hat-reviver and dog-stealer, in his dismallest tones.

That ill-used individual had not been killed, thanks to the thickness of his skull; the bullet from Lady Augusta's pistol had merely grazed his forehead — stunning him so effectually, however, that he remained where he fell till the servants, who hurried to the spot on hearing a rather incoherent report of the encounter from their youthful mistress, found him stretched, apparently lifeless, on the carpet.

When he recovered consciousness, one policeman was solicitously undoing his neck-cloth, and another, with equal tenderness, binding a cloth over his bleeding face, from which the black mask had been torn with very little ceremony.

Mr. Bunce eyed his pals lugubriously, and then the strangely-attired company that had gathered in a circle at a respectful distance, with a thoroughly ill-used and misanthropic expression.

"Here's a sittivation," he added, in the same sepulchral voice, "for a respectable tradesman what kept his own wehicle! Arn't it enuff to haggrawate a hangel? And it's hall a howing to that sanguinary Bishop o' Bond Street, who tuk my bread hout of my mouth, when I was a restoring o' lost dogs to their bereavèd howners."

Lord Cassington looked curiously at the melancholy burglar; and his sister, who had slid her hand into his the moment she came up to him, felt him start.

The Viscount led her away with mingled feelings of disgust and horror. She looked up into his face with a mournful yet tender expression. She was not thinking of the ruffian at all, or of the fright he had given her; she cared to think only that her favourite brother was unharmed.

"Why didn't you scream, Pussy?" he said, placing his hand fondly on her disordered hair, "when you first discovered that miscreant in the library? I would have rushed to your assistance in a moment."

"Would you, Cass?" she said, softly; and her pale face flushed with pleasure. "But I thought perhaps you might come to grief, and —and—I knew I could defend myself."

"You're a brave girl, my pet, and possess an affectionate, tender, womanly heart, notwithstanding some queer ways you have."

"I wouldn't have any queer ways if you didn't like them, Cass?"

He stooped down and kissed her. They were at the foot of the grand staircase.

"You're a trump, Pussy, if ever there was one."

"I'm glad you think so," she replied, her

eyes flashing proudly, as she took a chamber candlestick with a wax light he had lighted for her with a lamp he had brought from the steward's room.

"But you must promise me to go to bed, my dear child. The police are taking those scoundrels away by the back entrance. Some of the servants will assist in conveying them to the lock-up in the neighbouring town, and in half an hour the house will be as quiet as usual."

"I don't suppose that I shall be able to sleep, Cass. I cannot help thinking of your going away, after I have been so jolly with you as far back as I can remember."

"It can't be helped, Pussy, and we'll be more jolly than ever when I return."

"But I don't want you to go," she answered, impatiently, the tears starting to her eyes. "What's the use of your going among those horrid Turks, I should like to know—a set of Blue Beards who put ladies into sacks, and then fling them into the sea."

"Did your governess tell you that solemn fact, my pet?"

"Oh, bother my governess!" cried the

young lady; then, with a hasty "Good-night!" she ran lightly up the stairs, and did not stop till she re-entered her own chamber, where she knew she could indulge her feelings of regret unchecked.

The Viscount turned back to seek his brother. He met him in company with the Marquis, who had contrived to find his way to the scene of action just as the burglars were starting on their road to prison. Having ascertained that his plate was safe, and that no harm had come to any member of the establishment, the patrician Paterfamilias could afford to look at the affair from a facetious point of view; and was returning to bed in high spirits.

CHAPTER III.

FURNISHED LODGINGS.

"Goodness gracious, mamma, how it rains!"

This exclamation came from the Honorary Secretary of the South Pimlico Ragged School, as she came close to the parlour window of the respectable lodging-house in the bye-street in Belgravia. It was a favourite post of observation for that philanthropic spinster, between light and dark. When she could not see to perform what she somewhat grandiloquently styled her official duties, she could observe the goings on of her opposite neighbours, which, in truth, was a recreation both with her and her respectful parent, the manager's widow.

"I don't suppose we shall have visitors to-night, Clarissa," replied Mrs. Bootles, who was employed in putting the tea equipage together that had just been used, ready for removal by the small maid-of-all-work, who had only gone out a minute, and had been half an hour giggling with the baker's apprentice at the corner shop.

"Perhaps not, mamma. But goodness gracious! there's another disturbance at No. 9."

Mrs. Bootles hastened to the window in a lively state of excitement. No. 9 was the *bijou* of a furnished house, to which reference has several times been made in these volumes, and had long been a source of the most lively curiosity to the estimable ladies who lived opposite.

"What can that creature be about now, I wonder?" cried the mother, peering close to the panes, across the wet street. "I awoke very early, disturbed by a noise, and peeping under the window, saw her in all her finery on her door-step, absolutely squaring up to the cabman who had brought her home. It was then five o'clock in the morning. She wouldn't pay him his fare, and abused him in the most violent language I ever heard."

"And at ten, mamma, while I was getting breakfast, the dirty man who is always hanging about there, went out with the milk jug, and I watched him into the public-house at the corner; and Mary says the barmaid told her that he has half a pint of gin there twice a day, and sometimes more."

"Shocking! And the creature so young too. But what can the wretch be making such a noise about?"

Mrs. Bootles, whose inquisitive spirit was quite as powerful as her daughter's, quietly undid the fastening of the window, and let down the top. The sound of a shrill female voice was now heard distinctly.

"Do you hear that, mamma?"

"Yes, dear."

"*I'll let you know what I'm made of!*"

The words were screamed out so powerfully that any mistake about them was out of the question.

"I wonder whether the gentleman is there?" said Miss Bootles, inquiringly.

"Yes, Clarissa, I saw him jump out of a Hansom."

"What, the handsome young man with the long whiskers?"

"Yes. He's been away some time, you know."

"It's a pity, mamma. He is evidently aristocratic. Only noblemen wear such beautiful whiskers."

"*I'll let you know what I'm made of!*" was again screamed out in the same shrill tones.

"I dare say the wretch is intoxicated."

"Mary says the servant at No. 8 told her that the scenes lately enacted there have been dreadful. Scarcely a day passes without her making a disturbance. Her master has threatened to indict the house."

"Very proper. If this isn't put a stop to, the street will become quite disgraceful."

Various exclamations were heard, of anything but a feminine character, evidently proceeding from a woman in a violent passion. Presently there were sounds as of a scuffle in the passage. The street door opened, and a gentleman was violently thrust into the street by a slight female figure in a smart silk dress, her hair tumbling about her face, and that face bearing the aspect of a drunken fury. The door was then violently banged, and she disappeared.

"Goodness gracious, mamma; the creature's turned him out, and it's absolutely pouring cats and dogs!"

The rain was falling in a torrent, flooding the gutters, smoking the pavement with the violence and heaviness of its fall, and filling the road with splashing puddles and floating mud. Nevertheless, the expelled visitor from the *bijou* of a furnished house, though only lightly clad, quietly unfurled a silk umbrella, and stood as close under the doorway as he could squeeze himself, smoking a cigar, with as little emotion on his handsome face as if his new position was quite an every-day affair.

The street was deserted, and he was not aware that he was observed. Indeed, if he had noticed Mrs. and Miss Bootles it would not have troubled him in the least. He smoked on with an air of profound philosophy. He might have admitted that the thing was a bore, but then he was too used to bores to let any of them put him out of temper.

When he had nearly smoked out his cigar he flung the end into the spluttering gutter, stretched out his arm over the railings, and knocked with his fingers against the parlour window.

"Kitty! Kitty! My pet of pets, open the door?"

"Do you hear that, mamma?"

"Yes, Clarissa, and am certainly very much astonished!"

"When such a creature uses him in so brutal a way! Why, I wouldn't turn a dog in the street on a night like this, much less a nobleman!"

"He deserves all he gets, my dear. If young men of fashion condescend to such society, they ought not to complain if they are treated worse than dogs."

"Kitty! Kitty! Let me in!"

There was no response to either appeal. For a very good reason. The mistress of the house, having thus disposed of her visitor, reeled back to the sofa, on which she threw herself, and was the next minute totally unconscious of all external objects.

The patience of the gentleman on the door step was not exhausted, nor his good-nature, nor his stock of cigars. He lit another Havannah under his umbrella, and smoked with great apparent comfort in the midst of the deluge. He tapped at the window pane over and over again; he called in the most amiable manner for admission; but when he discovered that his thin boots were beginning to feel the influence of the moisture, and became aware that he was near the conclusion of his last cigar, he hailed an empty Hansom that was passing through the bye-street to the railway station, sprang down the sloppy door step and the floating pavement, and was immediately proceeding at a rapid pace to his club in Pall Mall.

Mrs. and Miss Bootles apparently much edified by what they had seen and heard, and satisfied that they were not likely to see or hear anything more, equally edifying, closed the window and the shutters, and returned to their seats. The small maid had not yet returned from her very short errand. Probably the rain detained her, but more likely she had not exhausted her stock of gossip. Be this as it may, the two ladies sat by the fire-light, with their hands before them, in a state of easy gentility and calm respectability, corresponding with the amount of their independence.

"I am afraid human nature has become very desperate," observed the manager's widow, "at least in this neighbourhood. The spectacle we have just witnessed is only one sad proof how little good is effected by the attempts so laudably made here for the diffusion of spiritual instruction."

"Yes, mamma! It's enough to dishearten any one cultivating philanthropic sentiments on true church principles, to notice the unparalleled disappointments and vexations of one's daily experience of degenerate human nature. There was that wretched man who imposed on us as a Polish patriot—that was very disheartening!"

"Very!" exclaimed Mrs. Bootles, feelingly.

"And this very morning as I was going to the school I discovered one of the brigade, whom I had been making a pet of as a model Ragged Boy, playing at marbles with a sweep, instead of following his profession. And he was swearing awfully!"

"It's very disheartening, indeed! It really costs a great deal, and the bulk of the expense falls upon us—for the Curate says he cannot divert the offertory money any longer to such a purpose."

"I don't think Mr. Corbel very zealous, mamma!"

"I've no doubt he's zealous enough with ladies of title," observed the manager's widow, like an indignant Lady Teazle. "Humbler churchwomen, my dear, however useful, are not thought so worthy of his attentions, you may depend on it."

"He hasn't come in with the latch-key for ever so long."

"Yet I saw him with my own eyes yesterday opening the door of No. 2. But then the eldest Miss Pinnock is considered very good looking, my dear."

Mrs. Malaprop could not have looked the sarcasm more effectively.

"I cannot see anything to admire in her, mamma. She is too fond of dress, too, by agood deal. Yesterday she changed her gown three times and her bonnet twice."

"Weak-minded men, my dear, like to see handsome young women handsomely dressed, and Miss Pinnock knows this."

Mrs. Haller might have said this sentence, so serious was the tone.

"I do not think much of Mr. Corbel's sermons, mamma, do you?"

"No, my dear, the young man, in my estimation, has very little talent as a preacher. Light hair, with a pink and white complexion, are not attractive to me, my dear, particularly when in a pulpit."

The last words were uttered with the tragic solemnity of a Lady Macbeth.

"Now, there is one clergyman who realizes my idea of what a great preacher ought to be."

"Mr. Mordecate, Clarissa?"

"Yes, mamma! when you and I went last to his chapel, I cannot tell you how much I was impressed with the earnestness of his manner and the grace of his delivery. His voice was so exquisitely sweet, his language so charmingly convincing. Then his wonderfully expressive features, and his grandly-noble figure, mamma! Besides, his chapel is so sweetly pretty!"

At the close of this gushing speech, the lock of the street door was heard to turn, and the estimable women suddenly sat upright in their chairs, and composed their features, anticipating a clerical visitor. Presently the parlour door opened, and they were doomed to another disappointment, for the small maid entered the room. She was eloquent in excuses for her prolonged stay, but as the rain seemed quite sufficient to account for her absence, no notice was taken of it. She removed the tea-things and brought in the lamp almost in silence.

Mrs. and Miss Bootles now produced their work, and sat themselves down to it with their customary devotion to their official duties.

"I should think our lodger would soon want her tea, mamma."

The elder lady looked at the time-piece, and quietly acquiesced.

"It was very good of Mr. Fairholme to recommend her to us!" suggested her daughter, but without glancing up from the flannel she was diligently sewing.

"Yes, Clarissa. It was very good of him, I dare say. But, to tell you the truth, I do not quite like her story."

"No more do I, mamma!" exclaimed the diligent sempstress.

"She's married, and yet she's not exactly a wife. And then, you see, she's very handsome. Clergymen are so easily imposed upon, my dear, by designing women; Mr. Fairholme is a very good young man, to all appearance; but then the best of men are but men, Clarissa, when a pretty face attracts them."

This oracular sentence was emphasized as if spoken by Hamlet's mother to her philosophic son.

"It's very mysterious, certainly."

"I do not quite like it. It seems as if we were about to compromise ourselves by harbouring a young person of whom we know very little."

"Yes, mamma!"

"Our position in good society ought not to be lightly hazarded; and then, my dear, we are bound to bear in mind our moral responsibilities."

The manager's widow uttered this opinion slowly and deliberately, in exactly the tones she had employed years before, when she played principal tragedy and comedy in her husband's theatre.

"I quite agree with you, mamma! but hadn't we better give her notice to quit?"

"No, my dear!" was answered hurriedly, "not so long as she pays her rent regularly."

This climax was singularly impressive in its delivery. It would have been a point had it been uttered on the boards of the Theatre Royal, Bagnigge Wells.

"I should not like to offend Mr. Fairholme by doing anything harsh to a person in whom he chooses to take an interest, and, as yet she has given no cause of offence. No one has called upon her but the lawyer, and her conduct has been very quiet—indeed, perfectly irreproachable. So there can be no necessity for getting rid of her at present. By the way, I think I will go up to her myself, and see if she wants anything. We have no right to condemn any one without proof, whatever we may think."

"No, mamma! we ought not to be hasty. 'Judge not, lest ye be judged' was the text of Mr. Mordecate's beautiful sermon last Sunday. By the way, mamma, do you know what is being done to No. 6. Men have been at work there more than a week, and Mary says she heard that it was going to be turned into a religious institution. I asked Mr. Corbel, after the tea-party to the school-children, but he didn't seem to know anything about it."

"Mr. Corbel never seems to know anything except the way to Miss Pinnock's, my dear," said the matron, putting aside her work. "I doubt whether he'll very quickly forget that. The house in question is undergoing a thorough repair, perhaps. It belongs to Peters and Binks, the auctioneers and land agents, who may probably have found a tenant for it. Not much reliance is to be placed on Mary's gossip. The street, my dear, I am afraid, is going down rapidly. Nearly all the houses have been taken by speculating butlers and housekeepers who have saved money, to turn into lodging-houses. If this goes on much longer we shall be obliged to leave it. I do not like such intensely domestic neighbours, Clarissa."

The manager's widow sailed out of the room as if she was going off at the wings, having delivered "a tag" of the most telling character. Leaving her daughter to the undisturbed possession of her own speculations and the work-table, she mounted the neatly-carpeted stairs, and ascended to the drawing-room floor, at the door of which she paused and knocked.

The permission to enter having been given, she turned the glass handle of the door, opened it, and advanced over the Brussels carpet with an assumption of grave decorum and genteel affability, worthy of herself, her position, and her moral responsibility.

She saw at a glance that there was no one in the room but her lodger, who appeared absorbed with the contents of an open letter, that must have come that day by the foreign post. She saw also at a glance, that everything else in the apartment was in its place—including the five-pound mirror over the fire-place, the portrait of the deceased manager on the opposite wall—the maple-framed prints of the religious charity-girls, and the attentive chorister boys over each recess, her best easy-chair, in which her lodger was seated, the two card-tables in the recess, the half-dozen rose-wood chairs, the walnut-wood piano, the Pembroke table, the muslin sweeps, the rug, carpet, and the fire-irons, even the ornaments on the mantelpiece—one and all exactly where she wished them to be.

Lady Vallance raised her head, and recognized her landlady, looking a concentration of gentility and goodness of heart. The former at once apologized for her apparent inattention, not expecting any one but the servant, and then observing that her visitor had closed the door behind her, asked her to be seated.

"I am exceedingly sorry to have disturbed your ladyship," cried Mrs. Bootles, with exaggerated regret. "But I hope you have received good news."

"Yes, Mrs. Bootles. I wrote to my uncle in Italy, stating my case, and asking permission to return to him, and he has written to apprise me, that he has been interesting himself in my affairs, and is about to sail for England, the better to enable him to be of service to me."

"The worthy man! The estimable creature! What an excellent uncle he must be!"

The manager's widow sat herself down before her lodger in an apparent ecstacy, and with a decided inclination to learn as much as she could respecting this convenient kinsman, who was going to turn up at so seasonable a moment.

"Of course he is very well off, Lady Vallance."

"Yes, Mrs. Bootles, Captain Mauleverer has realized a large fortune."

"How very gratifying that must be to you, my Lady. Permit me to do myself the honour to congratulate your ladyship on your ladyship's decidedly agreeable prospects."

"Thank you, Mrs. Bootles."

"Is there anything I can do to render your ladyship more comfortable?"

"No, thank you; I am quite contented, and am well pleased to have found so quiet a retreat."

"Rest assured that all shall be done to render it agreeable to you. May I ask, my Lady, when your ladyship expects the gentleman? I did not catch his name."

"Captain Mauleverer."

"Captain Mauleverer; thank you, my Lady, a most respectable name. And he will be in London——"

"In a few days."

"Thank you, my Lady. Would he require apartments in the same residence as your ladyship?"

"Oh no. He would stay at an hotel."

"Thank you, my Lady. Of course; how foolish I must be to think my humble domicile could furnish adequate accommodation for a gentleman of his resources. He will probably stop at the Palace Hotel, or the Brunswick, or the Clarendon."

"My uncle tells me that he shall stay at the White Horse Cellar, in Piccadilly, where he always stops when he visits London."

"The White Horse Cellar, in Piccadilly!" exclaimed the manager's widow, in great apparent astonishment, Captain Mauleverer from a star, sinking, in her estimation, to a walking gentleman. "Pardon me if I make the remark, that the near relative of a lady of title, ought to be more regardful of appearances."

"My uncle is perfectly able to judge for himself the kind of place he should prefer as a temporary residence."

"Oh! of course, my Lady," cried Mrs. Bootles, feeling herself snubbed. "And wealthy gentlemen are so very eccentric, especially elderly gentlemen, Lady Vallance."

"Captain Mauleverer ought not to be considered old, Mrs. Bootles."

"Oh indeed! young-looking, I suppose?"

"No, decidedly middle-aged, but in the prime of life—full of health and vigour."

"A most charming person, I have no doubt, my Lady. But as Captain Mauleverer is rich, and has moreover been in the habit of honouring the White Horse Cellar with his presence, it is very natural that he should prefer it to the fashionable hotels."

"My uncle wishes me to consult the Reverend Emanuel Mordecate," observed her lodger, looking at a passage in the foreign post letter.

"Mr. Mordecate!" cried her landlady, in unfeigned surprise. "Why he is the popular preacher at the Roman Catholic Chapel."

"Yes; Captain Mauleverer says he is a priest. He knew him when he was in Rome."

"How very strange!"

"Could I see the reverend gentleman by calling at the chapel? or had I not better write to apprise him of my uncle's wish that I should receive the benefit of his advice? I think I will write, Mrs. Bootles."

"As your ladyship pleases. I am not certain that Mr. Mordecate is at the chapel, or even in London, for I have not heard of his having preached for the last two or three weeks; but any communication from your ladyship, would of course be conveyed to him with all possible celerity, and should he be within reach, there can be no doubt of his hastening to pay your ladyship a visit."

"Then I think I will write at once, Mrs. Bootles."

Lady Vallance took a little desk from one of the card-tables and placed it before her. The manager's widow was too well-bred to remain. She rose, and seemed about to take her departure. She waited for the little desk to be opened, but saw nothing that rewarded her curiosity.

"Shall I send Mary up with the tea-things, my Lady?"

"In five minutes, Mrs. Bootles."

"I have the honour of wishing your ladyship good evening."

"Good evening, Mrs. Bootles."

The lodger did not move her eyes from the note-paper on which she began to write her address, and the landlady's faultless exit was quite unobserved.

"It's very mysterious!" she thought to herself, as she descended the stairs. "*Captain* Mauleverer! a good-looking uncle and rich, who is not at all old, coming from Italy to visit a lady of title who wants to get rid of her husband—a man of very bad character and poor—and then a Popish priest who has the reputation of being a Jesuit, is to be added to the *dramatis personæ*. These are the elements of a comedy of real life, that would unquestionably have drawn money into the treasury, as an after-piece."

"Well, mamma!" cried Miss Bootles, looking up from her charitable work, as her parent entered with a very perplexed face. "Goodness gracious! has anything happened?"

"I don't know what to think, Clarissa!" replied the elder lady, sinking into her seat like Queen Catherine, after an interview with Cardinal Wolsey.

"Think about what, mamma?"

"Lady Vallance has a rich uncle coming to her from Italy, who is not in the least old-looking—a *Captain* Mauleverer!"

"Goodness gracious!"

"And she is now writing a letter to that handsome Roman Catholic clergyman, the Reverend Emanuel Mordecate."

Miss Bootles threw up her hands and eyes in amazement. "Oh, mamma! what shall we do?"

"I haven't the least idea. I never felt so mystified in my life. One really does not know what to do for the best. I have not the slightest cause of complaint. Her conduct is perfectly irreproachable. She has been recommended to me by a clergyman of blameless character—and my dear——"

"What, mamma!"

"She pays her rent as regular as clockwork."

There was a silent pause of a few minutes.

"We must wait and see what sort of a person is this *Captain* Mauleverer, and how she conducts herself when he arrives."

"Yes, mamma."

"And we must see what she will do with the handsome clergyman."

"Yes, mamma."

This decision having been come to, seemed satisfactory to both, and they worked on with their usual industry, without again referring to the subject.

CHAPTER IV.

FOX HUNTING.

A WONDERFUL stir of human life reigned throughout the Hall, from its respectable proprietor to the smallest of those small boys who had offered their valuable services to the head-groom or the house-steward. Every one seemed imbued with a new spirit, which demonstrated itself in intense activity, and in an assumption of prodigous importance. Something wonderful must have happened. The establishment was totally different from what it had been, and there was as decided a change in the master.

Mr. Drelincourt had hitherto since his retirement from the great Bristol firm, been content with the assumption of a modest degree of importance, as a subordinate member of the landed aristocracy of the kingdom, a quiet imitator of that picturesque type of the English country gentleman whose portrait honest Dick Steele had introduced to the notice of the *belles* and *beaux* of the stately Court of Queen Anne; but, as in innumerable similar instances, the appetite had grown with what it fed on.

Since his visit to Mount-Trevor Court, and his acquaintance with the county magnates, the attractiveness of the one great object of his hero-worship appeared to diminish. He had been put forward as the representative of the county; he had seen himself named in the newspapers as one of the persons likely to be selected by the Crown to fill the responsible office of High-Sheriff; he had been appointed a Deputy-Lieutenant, and put in Commission of the Peace.

He had been gazetted as Colonel of the Blankshire Volunteers; he had been advertised as President of the United Blankshire Odd Fellows; he had been voted Perpetual Grand of the Royal Blankshire Free and Accepted Masons; he had become a Patron of the

Blankshire Athenæum and Mechanics Institute, and a Governor of the Blankshire Royal Lying-in Hospital and General Infirmary.

In brief, under the auspices of Lord Mount-Trevor, and the county magnates, including the Bishop's lady, he had subscribed to everything in the most liberal manner possible, and in the most liberal way had been invested with all the provincial honours that could be accumulated on his honoured head, or more truthfully speaking upon his honoured pocket.

In this way he was recommending himself to the county constituency. Much, however, as he had been doing, he was well aware that there was much more to be done. He had determined to be the most popular man in that part of the United Kingdom, and although the *Blankshire Telegraph* had for the last week been assuring its readers that this was already the case, the leaders of the *Blankshire Guardian* had been ridiculing the presumption of the new man, and kindly recommending him to go back to his Bristol warehouses before the enlightened freeholders of that most important county made him an object of universal ridicule.

Finding that a strong party were straining every nerve to drive him from the field, Mr. Drelincourt threw into the contest all that energy and enterprise with which he had so successfully conducted his enormous mercantile transactions. He sought to render himself acceptable to every one who possessed a vote, without the slightest reference to his political opinions; and, as the first move in this direction, made the Hall a house of entertainment for the entire county.

One day he gave a breakfast to the Hunt; the next day he had an Archery Meeting for the United Toxopholites; the third he gave a banquet to the Volunteers; the fourth he had a tea-party for the High-Church friends of the Bishop's lady; the fifth a ball for the fashionable and very genteel families, under the auspices of the Marchioness; and on the sixth he entertained the Agricultural Society, which included all the well-to-do farmers who possessed a vote.

The establishment at the Hall had been largely increased, and the importance of its members had kept pace with the pretensions of their employer. They were too well paid not to be satisfied with their position, and made their satisfaction no secret in the neighbourhood. In addition, Mr. Drelincourt employed a large number of labourers, not only on his extensive improvements, but in mining works he had commenced on an extensive scale, with the approval of the most eminent professors of mineralogy and mining agents he could consult, and under the superintendence of Professor Grauwacke, whose services he had engaged at a handsome salary.

Notwithstanding the personalities of the editor of the *Blankshire Guardian*, and the decided opposition of the party of which that journal was the organ, the retired merchant was steadily winning golden opinions in all directions. The day of nomination was approaching, and he exerted himself to make another great gathering of the principal voters, to recommend himself further to their good offices.

With this object in view there was a meet of the Blankshire Foxhounds in the vicinity of "the Hall," for the purpose of drawing the covers on the estate, and a great field had assembled, partly in anticipation of unusual sport, partly in expectation of the great Hunt Dinner which "the Squire," as he was now generally styled, had announced was to terminate the day's sport.

Mr. Drelincourt had donned a new velvet cap, a pink coat, indeed a first-rate hunting turn out, for this occasion, and had purchased two or three powerful hunters, at an enormous price, that had been warranted master of his weight. When he appeared at the Meet riding by the side of his beautiful daughter, he was cheered lustily. Probably the young lady came in for a considerable share of this demonstration, for she looked very attractive in her habit and feathered hat, moreover was known far and wide to be the best match in the county.

The scene was very animated, for, in addition to the large assemblage of horsemen, there were several carriages full of ladies drawn up near the cover side, and a sprinkling of fair equestrians doing their very best to look both handsome and interesting—talking and laughing in the most cheerful manner possible, and dispensing glances and smiles with as much discretion as amiability.

Some horses pranced about a good deal, especially those ridden by the younger members of the Hunt, but whether to show off their own valuable points or the equitation of their riders, was open to question. Sometimes one would dash across the field towards a group, probably acquaintances; presently another would rear up in rather an alarming manner to the young ladies who were near, but without doing the slightest injury to the young gentleman on his back.

Amicable sportsmen would bring their faces together to light their cigars; and communicative ones would appear extremely confidential as they kept their impatient chargers as close to each other as they could get them. Then there was a great display of familiar shouting, shaking hands, laughing, and demonstrations of good-fellowship generally, every one endeavouring to be jocose and jolly, and wonderfully good-natured, and ready to put his horse at anything. The county magnates were condescending and intensely patronizing, and the respectable young farmers full of dash, independence, and pleasantry.

"My dear fellow!" cried the Marquis, riding up to his neighbour with more even than his usual affability. "Allow me to compliment you on your appearance. And you've got a good horse, too! that is, if he can go as well as he looks!"

"I'll try his pace, presently, my Lord," replied Mr. Drelincourt, smiling, and evidently quite content with his purchase.

"Ah, Miss Drelincourt!" exclaimed Lord Mount-Trevor, taking off his hat with that tender courtesy for which his advances to pretty women had always been characterized. "Your appearance sets my complimentary powers at defiance. All the young fellows are in raptures about you, and some of the old fellows, too, if I'm not mistaken. Drelincourt, the Duchess wants to speak to you. She's standing up in the phæton beside the Duke."

Mr. Drelincourt rode his magnificent horse in the direction indicated by his obliging friend, who merely wanted to get rid of him, for the Duke and Duchess of Blankshire he had reason to regard as his most valuable allies.

"Now, Miss Drelincourt, with your permission," added the Marquis, "we will go to Lady Mount-Trevor, who, indeed, sent me to fetch you. Happy fellow I ought to think myself, when I see around me so many much more desirable escorts envying me my good fortune."

The message of the Marchioness the heiress felt bound at once to obey, and smiling at the good-natured messenger she prepared to canter across the turf towards the Mount-Trevor carriage. But the good-natured messenger had invented the message. All he wanted was to be seen by the field as the chosen escort of that highly popular young lady. And he rode by her side looking intensely satisfied with his *bonne fortune*, facetiously winking now and then in a manner some of his contemporaries thought exceedingly provoking.

"I am glad to see you looking so well, my dear," was the greeting she received from the Marchioness, as she reined up at the open carriage. "It is a great pity that Lionel is not here! I am sure that he would be very much pleased with your appearance!"

The heiress looked grateful, and felt so as she eagerly pressed the gloved hand held out to her; but her heart was heavy notwithstanding the interest she felt in the exciting scene around her. Lord Lionel's absence had been prolonged far beyond what she had expected would have been its limit; as a very natural result she had become uneasy at its duration and dissatisfied with its cause.

"If Lionel is not here I hope I may be considered a respectable substitute," said the Marquis, gallantly. "And I'm sure I'm quite as much pleased with Miss Drelincourt's appearance as he could be."

The heiress tried to answer the little amiable laugh of the beautiful Marchioness.

"Lionel has gone as far as Malta with his brother," added the latter. "They started yesterday from Southampton."

"And he did not think it worth while to write to me," thought his affianced, with a visible increase of her dissatisfaction.

"Now, gentlemen, 'ware hounds, if you please," cried a strong voice.

The hounds had been turned into one of the covers. A considerable interval had elapsed, which some of the Meet had engaged in watching,—the majority in gossiping. When the expected cry arose from the coppice, very few except the huntsman and whipper-in seemed to be aware that the fox had been found; and when he broke cover almost among them, there was a confusion in the riders nearest the pack, that looked alarming to those who observed it at a distance.

"Keep back—keep back! 'Ware hounds, I say!" shouted the huntsman, in a much fiercer voice than before.

Miss Drelincourt's little mare became restless; this, however, might be said of almost every equine member of the numerous cavalcade. All seemed to have made up their minds for a rush to the front.

"'Ware hounds!" again shouted the huntsman, angrily, to the crowd of riders vainly endeavouring to restrain the impatience of their high-mettled steeds. Miss Drelincourt anxiously looked for her father, for the mare was beginning to curvet and rear in a manner anything but pleasant; but there was a mass of horsemen between her and the Duke of

Blankshire's carriage, that prevented her from seeing him.

"I think we shall lose nothing, Miss Drelincourt," said the Marquis, keeping as close to her as the very lively mare would permit, "if we remain where we are till we can ensure that desideratum to all adventurers—a clear field and no favour."

The heiress was quite content to abide by this advice; but the thorough-bred on which she was mounted was evidently of a different mind; and all her knowledge of equitation was forced into requisition to enable her to keep her saddle.

Lord Mount-Trevor encouraged her, and, like an attentive cavalier, kept a good look-out on the mare's movements, riding as close to her as he could get. He prided himself on his knowledge of horseflesh, almost as much as on his knowledge of glaciers, and he did not at all like the expression of the animal's eye. Her fair rider continued to pat her arched neck with a glove as soft as her satin coat, and soothe her with a multitude of endearing expressions, in what the Marquis confessed was a thoroughly lady-like voice; but, though a good horsewoman, Miss Drelincourt was beginning to feel nervous.

The fact is, her feelings had been tried by the unexpected intelligence she had received of her absent lover; and this, in conjunction with the exciting scene in which she found herself placed, deprived of the confidence she invariably experienced in her father's companionship, created an unpleasant flurry in her spirits.

They had, notwithstanding their disposition to remain where they were, advanced a considerable distance from the Marchioness, who was waving her lace handkerchief towards them. The field was rapidly thinning, the hounds, though with some difficulty, having been permitted to get off without accident, which was not the case with all the horsemen; for before a quarter of a mile had been traversed, one had contrived to get his head in contact with the branch of a tree, and had been sent backward on the grass—two had been deposited in a dry ditch, with their heels in the air—and a few more had been unhorsed by those mischances almost inseparable from a crowded Meet and a start in a rough line of country.

The heiress looked for her father in the direction in which she had last seen him; but though the space was clear, she could not distinguish his well-known figure anywhere.

"Now I think you had better give the mare her head," observed her companion. "Your father, no doubt, is somewhere in advance. He is well mounted, and, I have no doubt, will go straight after the hounds; but I should recommend you to keep in the park, because you would avoid some ugly fences over which they have passed, and be enabled to cut off a considerable distance, for the fox is evidently making for the warren."

Miss Drelincourt turned the mare's unwilling head towards an open gate, and cantered in that direction. It led through the home park, into what was called "the wilderness," —a wide stretch of open land, here and there broken by plantations. It had hitherto, in the summer months, been remarkable chiefly for its luxuriant growth of ferns and foxgloves, but the level had been disturbed in many places, and varying undulations were beginning to appear, covered with ornamental shrubs or carefully protected nurseries of young trees.

On the turf the canter of the mare shortly became a gallop, and the stride of the Marquis's hunter was increased, to enable that now most attentive of cavaliers to keep up with his charge. Affable and courteous as he had always appeared to the retired merchant's daughter, his lordship had never been so amiable as he was then appearing. His conversation was exceedingly entertaining—far more so than she had found the talk of most of the young men with whose companionship she had been obliged to be content in the hunting field. Lord Lionel, indeed, though always very agreeable when riding with her, had, she confessed, never been so amusing, as was his father that morning.

The Marquis, perhaps, would not have been quite satisfied with the estimate the heiress formed of him in that quarter of an hour's gallop, though it was unquestionably favourable.

"Lionel's papa was a very nice person," she thought, "and must have been a charming man at Lionel's age."

Nevertheless, his lordship continued his pleasant talk, in the fullest reliance on his experience of the *carte du pays* of a feminine heart, to find his way to it. His conversation was very sprightly, in all respects that of a man of the world disposed to regard everything from a facetious point of view, and gather amusement wherever he could.

Though a man of gallantry, he had not the slightest idea of cutting out his son, with the young lady whom he was honouring with his attentions. He could not have entertained such a thought for a moment. No man more appropriately could have sung—

> "Pleased let me trifle life away,
> And sing of love as I grow old."

But he had no notion of singing of love to Miss Drelincourt; probably he had just as little idea of growing old. He prided himself on being a model of a patrician Paterfamilias, and therefore could not reconcile himself to taking advantage of Lionel's absence to rob him of the affections of his mistress—of course not.

All he wanted was to satisfy himself that, when he chose to exert himself to please a pretty woman, he could distance all the young fellows likely to enter the lists against him;

and he fancied, as he noticed the glance brighten and the cheek flush, that he was perfectly successful.

They at last emerged from the park by a door in the paling, which one of the labourers opened, and found themselves on a moor of considerable extent. They looked to the right and to the left, but not a trace of hounds or huntsmen could they see.

"We had better skirt the park, and mount the hill yonder," said Lord Mount-Trevor; "we shall get a good view of the country there. They have probably met with a check."

The heiress had no alternative, so cantered easily in the direction indicated, and then rode slowly up the elevation; the Marquis, of course, making the most of his opportunity, and, in the genial laugh and good-humoured comments of his lovely companion, finding assurance of a prodigious success.

At the top of the hill, a magnificent panorama spread out before the equestrians; and one or two landmarks, which Miss Drelincourt eagerly recognized, made her acquainted with her exact position. The river, the churches, the mansions in the distance, were hailed as familiar friends; still more cordially was hailed the spectacle of the Hunt, a good way off, in the valley below—the hounds in full cry, with about a dozen horsemen in their immediate rear; and at a long distance came a straggling mass, including not a few horses without riders.

They were plainly to be seen; the best mounted or more adventurous dashing over every obstruction, whether of stream, fence, or hedge. Some sprawling, some tumbling, some running after steeds that had thrown them and got away, and several up to their necks in a deep brook they had ventured to cross.

The heiress viewed the stirring scene with a good deal of interest, her attentive companion acting showman from a decidedly facetious point of view, making immense fun of the people who were tailed off, had taken to grass, or were enjoying an involuntary bath. To do him justice, Lord Mount-Trevor was in great force, and it was impossible for Miss Drelincourt not to be amused, with such an intensely jocose Cicerone.

"You see, my dear Miss Drelincourt," observed his lordship, with a particular satisfaction, "how extremely judicious it was of me to take the line I did. It is not at all improbable, that had we followed with the rest, one or both of us might have been numbered with the unfortunates down below. I should have been inconsolable had you suffered in that way; and, of course, you would be so had I been the victim."

"I hope that my father has not been thrown!" exclaimed the young lady, rather to the disappointment of her gallant, who had anticipated a little generous sympathy." "I shall be very glad to get nearer the Hunt, for the chance of falling in with him."

The Marquis complied with a good grace, and they proceeded slowly down the hill. When the descent became more gradual, the horses appearing to recognize the cry of the hounds wafted to them by the breeze, pricked up their ears, and increased their pace. They presently came on level ground, and went at a gallop over the next field, which they entered by a gap in the hedge.

They soon came upon a much more difficult

country—meadows intersected by streams, turnip fields surrounded by broad ditches; sometimes a quickset hedge in addition, and ploughed lands skirted by deep lanes, with banks and broad ditches. The Marquis gallantly picked out the most accessible bit of paling, the broken hedge-row, or the narrowest ditch, and attentively encouraging his fair charge to take the leap, went over it in good style. Miss Drelincourt rose in her saddle as nearly as possible at the same time, lifting the mare a little, and passed the obstacle apparently with equal ease.

Immense was Lord Mount-Trevor's commendation as he witnessed the successful result of his suggestion, and his pleasantness became more and more facetious. Presently they came upon fences and streams more difficult to pass; but somehow, the light mare seemed to go over them more easily than the stout hunter. In a few minutes a gate barred the way, the heiress took it first clearly, but the Marquis smashed the top rail.

It should be borne in mind that the one rider was a particularly light weight, and the other not far off fifteen stone; the mare seemed almost as fresh as when she started; but the old hunter, though not exactly distressed, felt the effect of his ride to cover, and his longer ride since. His master, however, seemed every minute to increase in liveliness; nothing could exceed the freshness of his humourous fancy but the fertility of his facetious invention.

He was in a marvellous good humour—particularly with himself. It would be such a capital joke to tell at the club, when he returned to town, how he took away the lovely heiress from all the gallant youth of the county, and made himself immensely agreeable to her during one of the fastest runs in the season—brought her over the stiffest jumps he had attempted for many years; and he would, no doubt, triumphantly lead her up to the hounds, so that she should be in at the death, and get the brush.

But where were the hounds? O! they were within view, and by cutting right across country, he should be up with them before all the field—perhaps as soon as the huntsman and whipper-in, if the fox should swerve a little towards them. The idea delighted Lord

Mount-Trevor, and his exultation at his own cleverness was as great as his sense of his powers of pleasing.

"Now, my dear Miss Drelincourt!" he cried, looking almost as confident as he felt. "You've really been quite a Diana! Indeed, I very much doubt if that highly respectable young woman could have gone across country half as cleverly, even if she had got Endymion beside her to show her the leaps."

The heiress laughed, as she had done at all his lordship's gallant as well as facetious speeches, laughed musically, and looked delighted.

"We are now coming to a rather formidable jump," he added," but I'll bet you a dozen of gloves, I'll be over it first."

Miss Drelincourt did not reply, but prepared for the barrier of which she had received notice. It took the shape of an ox-fence, beyond which was a ditch. She immediately set the mare's head in the required direction, and, urging her on, with a tremendous rush, the animal sprung over it, and proceeded at the same pace across the field.

As she landed safely on the other side, the heiress turned her head round to observe how her companion got over, and saw his horse tumble backwards, his rider with him, into a broad ditch. Her first impulse was to turn back and go to his assistance, but the mare would not obey the rein. She had again heard the cry of the hounds, and increased her pace, despite the pulling of her rider.

Miss Drelincourt, finding that she had no power over her steed, though she strained at the reins with all her strength, began to feel alarmed. She did not know the neighbourhood, and the country bore a very rough and difficult aspect. She passed over a wild common at a terrific speed, and a sudden terror seized her, for she observed an embankment right before her, which, she suspected, overlooked a deep cutting of the railway. She held her seat, though her senses seemed about to leave her. Suddenly she heard some one shouting, and the clatter of horses' hoofs; but she did not dare look about her to see in what direction they were approaching.

Away sped the excited mare, apparently

with the bit in her teeth, and she was so closely approaching the embankment that destruction seemed inevitable. The heiress closed her eyes, and breathed a short but fervent prayer. The clatter of hoofs came nearer, but the sound seemed to madden the other horse to desperation, and she strained on in the same frightful course.

There was a rush as of a racer gaining the winning post, and as the mare came within a stride or two of the edge of the embankment, a firm grasp was laid on her bridle, her head was turned forcibly round, as another horse coming parallel with the line of the railway on the top of the embankment interposed between her and the precipice that divided both from the cutting.

Of course, this timely succour came from one of the sportsmen, following the hounds; or from one of those fearless young gentlemen who seem born only to save the lives of interesting young ladies who have contrived to get into danger. The reader will see presently.

"That's the cleanest shave I ever saw!" exclaimed a very pleasant voice.

Miss Drelincourt opened her eyes, with an impulse all young ladies in dreadful circumstances ought to have to thank their heroic deliverer, when she found occasion to open them very wide indeed.

"There's no occasion now to look frightened, Miss Drelincourt. You're as safe as a trivet!"

Still the heiress did stare rather wildly, and with her very pale face looked much as if she had seen a ghost. Her heroic deliverer was a girl, in a very pretty hat, and a still prettier jacket and skirt.

"I hope you are not going to faint, Miss Drelincourt, but you do look dreadful seedy. And no wonder either, for if I hadn't mounted Cass's Arab, and made him race as if he was winning the Derby, directly I caught sight of you going right into the cutting, *per Jupiter*, it would have been all U P with you."

"Lady Augusta! Can it be possible!"

"O nothing's impossible with me! I don't like possibilities, they're so awfully slow. I wish your mare would stand still. If I didn't hold her tight she'd be off again. I shouldn't recommend you to follow the Hunt further. I am afraid you're used up—at least for fox-hunting."

"Indeed I do feel ill. Perhaps I had better return home."

"All right, I'll settle it for you. You won't be able to manage the mare, but Cass's Arab is as docile as a lamb. There's a shepherd sitting yonder with his flock, let's ride gently up to him, and then you can dismount and ride the Arab. It will be uncommonly jolly for us two girls to ride home together, for, of course, you'll invite me to your crib, and I've been told there's to be no end of a spread there when the men come back from the Hunt. If we should be the only ladies present, wouldn't it be stunning?"

The heiress did not seem to know what reply to make to so strange a speech, but with the assistance of the shepherd—after first receiving a draught of spring water—she was able to exchange horses with her friend. Having seen Miss Drelincourt mounted, taking up her habit, Lady Augusta stood before the mare a few minutes, caressing her with her hand, looking into her eyes, and commending her good points with the fluency of a horse-dealer. Having in some degree calmed the animal's excitement, she sprung into the saddle without assistance. The mare made no resistance, and the two girls set off at little more than a walk.

"Holla! what awful Guy is this?" exclaimed Lady Augusta.

As they were crossing the common they beheld a very curious apparition. It was a gentleman in hunting attire, his hat crushed, one half of his red coat purple, the other black from a coating of slime, his white cords disfigured with large miry-green stains, his top-boots in a similar condition, and one half of his face bearing upon it a kind of crust, such as might belong to a dirt-pie, imperfectly baked.

"Who can it be, Lady Augusta?"

"*Per Jupiter!* it's my father!" she replied in a whisper.

It was the Marquis Mount-Trevor, but so terribly metamorphosed that no one but his own daughter could have known him, and she recognized the horse before she had suspected the identity of the rider. His lordship was no more like the facetious, the fascinating, the delightful Cicerone that he had been half an hour ago to the pretty heiress he had so cleverly carried off from the gallant youth of Blankshire, than was a drowned kitten like a Bengal tiger. His pleasantry had entirely evaporated, his gallantry totally disappeared. He hadn't a ghost of a joke to fling away upon the unfortunates who had been thrown out of the chase.

"Why, papa! what on earth has made you come to grief in this shocking way?"

The Marquis made a grimace. He would much rather have not met young ladies —particularly he should have liked to have avoided the pretty heiress—but he felt that there was no help for it; they had come upon him too suddenly for him to avoid them.

"Do you think the Hunt is taking this direction?" he asked.

"Yes, the fox is pretty sure of trying for the woods to run to earth," Lady Augusta replied, confidently. "In fact, you may see the pack now, just skirting the hill there, stern up and heads down, in full cry. They will be in this common in little more than a quarter of an hour, with all the field, that have been able to live the pace, cutting after them like old boots."

Lord Mount-Trevor made another grimace.

"I should prefer getting out of their way," he said solemnly. "I have an idea that my tumble has not improved my personal appearance, and I rather think that it would be conducive to my respectability as well as to my comfort, to make a change as soon as I can. It's a terrible bore."

"That's just it, and no mistake. So I should recommend you to disappear before any one sees your present highly picturesque aspect. Charley Forrester and his set would have no end of fun out of you, and there's that dreadful quiz, Lady Latimer. You know what awful sport she'd make of it."

The Marquis again indulged in a grimace. The thought of a recognition by such people was evidently not alluring. Like all facetious persons, prodigal of their jokes where other people's feelings were concerned, he was sensitive of a laugh against himself.

"But how did you get here, child?" he asked as he turned his horse's head, for the first time taking his attention from himself, "Your mamma told me that you would be occupied with your governess all the morning."

"Stole away, papa. After an hour or so, felt that I had had enough of that awfully slow party, so went to the stable and had Salem saddled for a little fresh air and exercise. Rode this way to get a glimpse at the chase. Saw a young lady whose horse was running away with her, put the Arab on her metal with the intention of saving this young lady from being carried over the highest embankment in all Blankshire, and by putting forth all my jockeyship, managed to interpose in the very nick of time. It was a precious near thing though, I can tell you."

"I'm delighted that you were of service to Miss Drelincourt. If my horse hadn't missed his footing on that bank, I am quite certain that she would have got well up to the Hunt without any mishap. It's a dreadful bore. I should have much liked to have returned with her to the Hall, but under the unpleasant circumstances of the case, if she will be so amiable as to excuse my further attendance——"

The young lady not only promptly excused his lordship, but expressed her regret for the accident that had deprived her of her escort.

Lord Mount-Trevor smiled in his most agreeable way, but unfortunately, this graceful addition to his features was hidden under a stratum of mud, and was therefore lost on the heiress.

"I say, papa!" cried Lady Augusta, as the Marquis took off his hat, which the heavy hoof of his horse had put singularly out of shape. "Make all right for me, with mamma. Say I couldn't leave Miss Drelincourt, who is really unable to ride the mare that run away with her; and please to be civil to my governess, for me, and explain satisfactorily my involuntary absence from school."

The Marquis made a grimace, but whether at the prospect of an explanation with the beautiful Marchioness, or with the severe spinster did not appear. He at once made his *adieux* in as gallant a manner as he could under most unfavourable circumstances, put spurs to his horse, and was presently lost to sight up a narrow lane that promised to screen him from observation.

Lady Augusta laughed heartily, as she turned the mare to cross the common into the high-road, which was then the most advisable way to take to the Hall.

"Poor papa, he will be in a terrible state of mind, till he makes himself presentable. But how are you now, dear? Do you feel fresh enough for a canter."

Miss Drelincourt acknowledged herself a little better, but was desirous of getting home as quickly as she could. Her companion saw that she still looked very pale, and considerately made the pace easy while endeavouring to amuse her by talking.

"It was uncommon plucky of Lionel to go with Cass, wasn't it?" she suddenly asked.

Miss Drelincourt's heart began to beat faster at the well-known name, and she realized the gratification of being alone with his sister, of whom she had previously seen very little. That young lady did not wait for an answer to her question.

"I think it so jolly that we are going to be sisters," she added.

Miss Drelincourt did not know what to think, but she felt very warmly towards the brave-hearted girl. She put out her hand with an affectionate look. Lady Augusta grasped it firmly.

"I think Lionel a lucky fellow, for anybody can see that you're a brick."

The heiress did not quite understand her young friend's meaning, but was satisfied that she intended to be friendly as well as complimentary, and smiled as if perfectly content with the somewhat ambiguous opinion.

"Some men, you know, would care only for your tin—but Lionel isn't that sort of creature at all. He used to rave about you awfully, I remember."

"Did he?" inquired her friend, a faint flush of pleasure passing over her pale cheek.

"And no mistake! You were first favourite. He was ready to back you at any odds, against the field."

"I did not know that he was so fond of betting."

"My dear Miss Drelincourt, you misunderstand me!" cried Lady Augusta. "All I meant to say was, that he estimated you far above all the young ladies he had seen."

The heiress had entertained doubts on this subject, but this assurance from so trustworthy a source was very gratifying to her.

"Are you quite certain, my dear Lady Augusta?" she inquired, timidly.

"Quite. To be sure he was once smitten with a girl he had seen at Florence, and I believe was rather soft upon her—but that ended in smoke, and I saw at once that when he became acquainted with you, it was a serious affair, and that he'd cut the other connection entirely."

Miss Drelincourt felt not only pleased but benefited by this communication. She seemed to be recovering her good spirits.

"Suppose we push on a little faster," said her companion, who had not been unobservant of the favourable change. "If you should be well enough to appear at the dinner, won't we recompense ourselves for having been thrown out of the Hunt! I'll take a rise out of

Charley Forrester, if I get a chance

The heiress was anxious to please Lionel's sister, though not at all comprehending her intentions. She quickened her pace, and they were presently proceeding rapidly along the high-road leading to the Hall Lodge, leaving the Fox-hunt far behind them.

CHAPTER V.

THE ROAD TO POPULARITY.

WHEN the fox broke cover, the first thought of Mr. Drelincourt was for his daughter; but the inclination of the powerful horse he bestrode, as well as that of a good many more in his immediate neighbourhood, prevented him from crossing to the place where he had left her. He found himself obliged to go with the cavalcade, and when tolerably free from their pressure, could see nothing of her in any direction.

Knowing that he had left her in charge of Lord Mount-Trevor, who was quite competent to take care of her, he tried to reconcile himself to their temporary separation. He had a serious purpose in connecting himself with this Hunt. The freeholders were fox-hunters almost to a man, and some of them he knew had anticipated sport, not so much from a good run as a good laugh.

Those who had ridiculed his improvements, those who had made the most of his attempt to form a rookery, to facilitate deer-stalking and make salmon-fishing easy, promised themselves famous entertainment by the exhibition of a second Mr. Briggs in the hunting field; but Mr. Drelincourt knew very well what he was about.

Sir Charles Forrester and all the young swells of his acquaintance, who had mustered in irreproachable pinks and white cords at the Meet, were welcome to as much quizzing as they could get out of the opportunity. Then he recognized the editor of the *Blankshire Guardian*, who had got a mount from the stables of the opposition party, and was following the Hunt for the express purpose of making a screaming article out of the day's run.

It so happened that Mr. Drelincourt had practised riding from a youth. Instead of going like a tailor, as had been confidentially anticipated, he rode much better than most men of his age. Instead of appearing on a stiff cob or a safe old hack, he came on one of the most magnificent hunters in the field—a horse that the best judges amongst them could not help acknowledging would be cheap at any price. Some of his preparations were still more sportsman-like, but these they had to learn.

The young swells, on comparing notes on the disappointment the retired merchant had created by his faultless get-up, consoled themselves with a *derniere pensée.* He would never be able to manage the powerful animal he had somehow or other got hold of; they should see him thrown at the first bull-find or ox-fence; they must inevitably part company, and then it would be first-rate fun to ride over him, and hope that he was not very much hurt.

Of course, they did not wish him to break his collar-bone, or fracture his ribs, or even dislocate his shoulder; for he was by no means a bad sort of fellow, and that daughter of his was really no end of a nice girl; but then it couldn't be allowed that such a person should intrude himself, in the alarming way he had done, into the most select society of the county. They could not hear of it; moreover they were sure he would make himself ridiculous in the hunting field.

Notwithstanding these impartial prognostications, Mr. Drelincourt was not long in proving, to the satisfaction of his critics, that he could ride well to hounds. Most of them had had the advantages of a good start; but one after another he passed them by, not only going at a slapping pace, but taking his leaps as coolly as a riding-master in his own school.

Sir Charles Forrester and one or two first-rate steeple-chasers kindly led him over the most difficult line they could select; but the young baronet had just been deposited in a brook, when the heels of the powerful hunter rode by "the second Mr. Briggs" went beautifully over his head. The Hon. Capt. Mildrington, of the Grenadier Guards, toppled upon a five-barred gate, immediately after "the stout party" had left it clear for him; and that dashing, clever young Irishman, Lord Adolphus Fitz-Patrick, who could do anything, was craning at a hedge, when a sudden rush made him turn his head to see "that fellow Drelincourt" nodding to him as he rose in his stirrups, going over like a bird.

"He did, by Jove," cried Lord Adolphus a few minutes afterwards to his astonished friends. "A party of his weight to attempt such a leap astonishes me uncommonly, but to do it in that easy sort of way, you know; really, 'pon my honour now, it's the pluckiest thing I ever saw in my life."

Mr. Drelincourt went on, surprising many persons besides his lordship and his steeple-chase friends. His way of clearing his fences, as well as of going over the ground, was the theme of general admiration. He had caused a fresh horse to be placed conveniently for the course the Hunt was expected to take, and though he had to make a considerable *détour* for it, the manner in which the animal did his work allowed of his overtaking those who had fancied that he had been thrown out.

"Well done, Squire!" cried Charley Forrester, also on his second horse, as Mr.

Drelincourt came flying over a fence close to him. "I couldn't have supposed you were such a thorough fox-hunter. Why, that's as good a horse as the other."

Mr. Drelincourt nodded to the young Baronet, who looked a little refreshed by his bath, smilingly shouted a few words about the splendid run, and taking another leap into a deep land, was soon out of sight.

"The second Mr. Briggs isn't so like the first as I thought," said the Honourable Captain Mildrington, of the Grenadier Guards, who had caught his horse after a good deal of difficulty.

"Briggs!" echoed Lord Adolphus twirling his delicate moustache with a look of grave surprise, "I'll bet fifty pounds on that man against any other stout party you can find, to jump twenty hurdles, or to go over any line of country you like."

The bet was not accepted. The impossibility of finding another "stout party" capable of contesting in equitation with "such a plucky fellow as that," was at once acknowledged. The trio presently rode on, with a very different opinion of the Squire than they had started with.

He had by this time got far in advance of them, when he noticed, as he was crossing a grass field, a middle-aged little man, in a black coat, looking both tired and dusty, running about trying to catch a horse that had evidently not long since thrown him, apparently with some violence, as he limped painfully. Mr. Drelincourt at once rode to his assistance, caught the fugitive by the bridle, and brought him to his rider. He was the editor of the *Blankshire Guardian*. That gentleman looked a little discomforted, nevertheless he received a most hearty recognition, and, when he had remounted, got a cordial shake of the hand.

"I hav'n't time to improve the acquaintance now, my dear sir," said the object of at least a score of the most furious political attacks. "But of course I shall have the pleasure of your company at dinner."

The discomfited editor was trying to frame an excuse, but before he could find fitting words, Mr. Drelincourt had spurred his horse, and was out of hearing, after the hounds that were still at a considerable distance.

He followed them much in the same

style till he found it necessary to take a third horse, and with this animal it was that he was up with the huntsman and whipper-in, when the fox was killed, after one of the severest runs known in the county, and was presented with the brush as his due.

With this honour publicly displayed, he rode back to the Hall, receiving the congratulations of such of the field as had not been tailed off, when the chase became too severe for ordinary horseflesh, and no one gave them more earnestly than the young swells who had joined the Meet expressly to ridicule his horsemanship.

The retired merchant was exceedingly gratified with the success of his arrangements. His satisfaction, however, had one drawback, and that was his inability to gain any tidings of his daughter or of Lord Mount-Trevor—no one had seen them after the start. Knowing that both were well mounted, this seemed surprising to Mr. Drelincourt; but as the return of mishaps in the field did not include either, he felt satisfied that they had come to no harm.

On reaching the Hall he could learn nothing

about the Marquis, but was relieved on ascertaining that his daughter had returned home, and was with Lady Augusta in her boudoir. There he quickly proceeded, and was soon put in possession of the story of her escape, for which he was not slow in expressing his obligations; and on these he dwelt the more earnestly when he learnt that in seizing the run-away mare Lady Augusta had given her arm a severe wrench. This injury she had courageously concealed during her ride back, but the limb from the wrist had become so swollen and painful that she had been obliged to confess the truth, and was now lying helpless and faint upon the sofa.

Dr. Dallas had not only joined the Hunt, but was then in the house. In a few minutes he was examining the young lady's arm with his most professional face. He pronounced it a severe injury that demanded the utmost care and quietude, at which its restless owner winced more than at the pain his movement of it occasioned her. He advised that her ladyship should remain where she was for a few days, at which she expressed no objection whatever; but when he insisted that she should give up all idea of appearing at the Hunt dinner, the patient was less docile.

She did not like being disappointed of the fun she had promised herself, and particularly of the retaliation she had devised at the expense of Charley Forrester; but she soon saw there was nothing for it but submission. The Doctor was firm, Mr. Drelincourt backed his decision stoutly, and Miss Drelincourt was equally obdurate, though she promised to remain with her the whole evening. The young lady gave in at last, expressing her opinion that the thing was a dreadful sell.

Just before the dinner was announced, who should knock at the door of the room in which were the two girls, but the Marquis Mount-Trevor, fresh as a bridegroom, in a new hunting suit, and as smiling, facetious, gallant, and good-humoured as ever. His lordship had thought that if he remained away his disaster would be talked about; and as he knew the editor of the *Blankshire Guardian* had joined the Hunt, it would be sure of appearing at full length in his wretched paper, would of course be copied into the London journals, and then run the round of the Clubs.

So with his usual diplomatic ability, as soon as he returned to Mount-Trevor Court, he had a warm bath, purified his nobility and dressed it up anew, and then drove in the dog-cart to the Hall, in time for dinner, with a well concocted story of his horse falling lame. Hearing on his arrival of his daughter's accident, like a model patrician Paterfamilias, as he was, he lost no time in seeking her retreat, very much to her surprise as well as that of her companion.

"Ah, governor, is it you?" exclaimed the younger of the two, rather languidly for her. "Why you look so spruce. I should recommend your taking a tumble every day."

Lord Mount-Trevor made a grimace, to insinuate perhaps that he did not care to hear any allusions to his disaster, and asked very paternally after her injury—perhaps to show his affection—perhaps to change the subject.

"Oh! thank you, I'm as well as can be expected under the circumstances. Please to tell my maid to send me some toggery, as the Doctor says I'm booked here for several days. I would not have minded if he hadn't made me go without the Hunt dinner I had so set my heart upon."

Miss Drelincourt gave her gallant companion of the morning a cordial reception, and endeavoured to reconcile his paternal feelings to the necessary separation from his daughter, who, she assured him, should be as affectionately tended as if under his own roof. The Marquis smiled, and expressed a reply, half-paternal and half-facetious—an exquisitely adjusted equilibrium of his feelings as a modern Paterfamilias, and of his taste as a perfect man of the world, willing to render himself agreeable to a pretty woman. At last, having accomplished all the smiling and jesting and grimacing that the occasion warranted, he took his leave.

There is no necessity to describe at length the banquet that Mr. Drelincourt had provided for his sporting friends; we can only assure the reader that it quite realized the opinion Lady Augusta had expressed of it. Every one acknowledged it to be the most magnificent spread the county had ever enjoyed at the expense of a private individual.

Lord Mount-Trevor sat at one end of the

table, indulging his appetite and his imagination in turn; the first being of course directed against the viands so liberally provided—the latter against Charley Forrester and such of the county youth who happened to be within hearing. Marvellous was the ride he described with the pretty heiress, and splendid wâs the artistic manner in which he told of his horse falling dead-lame just as the mare bolted with her rider. Then came his relation of the terrible hair-breadth escape—that was his masterpiece.

To do them justice, the young men listened not only with entirely interrupted mastication, but with a thrill of horror as the Marquis dwelt on the perilous position of the two girls.

It was quite a sensational story, and when the race of life or death had been made the most of by the skilful narrator, delighted with the attention he was exciting, and he described the crowning feat of his heroic child, and the injury the slight limb had incurred in the shock, every one seemed to share the pain, and to regret that he had not been near enough to the spot to have saved the heiress, and taken double the amount of Lady Augusta's suffering.

Scarcely anything else was talked off at table but the heroism of the fair friends, and it was difficult to say which excited most sympathy, the heiress for the frightful death she had escaped, or Lady Augusta for the fearless way in which she had risked similar destruction, on the chance of saving her brother's *fiancée*.

A good deal was said about the Hunt; and the giver of the feas thad full justice done him as its hero. His praises were on every tongue, and when his guests ceased to commend the rider, they eulogized his horses. What a stud he must have! What a fortune he must possess! More than all—What a credit he was to the county!

No one was louder in such panegyrics than Sir Charles Forrester, unless it was the Honourable Captain Mildrington, and no one more eloquent in such commendation than the Honourable Captain Mildrington, unless it was Lord Adolphus Fitz-Patrick. In short, the steeple-racers were the most enthusiastic in Mr. Drelincourt's favour of any of the company, especially after the cloth had been removed, the wine had circulated briskly, and the health of their host had been proposed in an exceedingly neat speech by the Marquis Mount-Trevor.

Nevertheless, though this liberal amount of hero-worship was expended on the right man in the right place, there was as handsome an under-current of heroine-worship felt for the young ladies, who had so profoundly excited their sympathy. Again and again the terrible story was gone over, with additional particulars respecting the horse each had mounted; after hearing which no one would be satisfied till he had learned the principal features of their several toilettes.

Then they went back to the locality. Every one would ride over to look at it the next morning. All expressed a wish for an engraving of the scene—it would be such an interesting illustration of county history. It would be such a pleasant memorial of two of the most celebrated of the county beauties. An artist might make a good thing of a picture taken on the spot; an author might realize something handsome by publishing an account of this remarkable romance of real life; a dramatist might get up a sensation play, in which the fearful ride on the verge of the embankment would be rendered more effective than the water scene in "the Colleen Bawn."

Sir Charles Forrester was very conspicuous among these enthusiastic young men. Lady Augusta was something more than a favourite of his. He had known her from a child—in truth, he had helped her brother in developing her eccentricities, and in getting a little harmless fun out of her now and then. Her good humour had been as much appreciated as her originality. Hearing her so much praised, and believing that he knew more about her than any one in the room, he felt bound to appreciate her higher than any body.

He was not content with joining in the commendation; when he had drunk a good deal of wine he felt unusually eloquent, and insisted on making a speech; other young men, who had drunk quite as much wine, got up, and also insisted on making speeches: and when they had delivered themselves of a considerable number of disconnected sentences of a marvellously discursive character, it began to appear that they were anxious to propose the healths of Miss Drelincourt and Lady Augusta Leigh.

Each orator had his knot of supporters, who cheered his confused utterances, and encouraged his husky declamation, till each having exhausted his oratory or feeling an overpowering inclination for his seat, suddenly sat down, when the applause very much increased.

It was while the fun was thus getting fast and furious at one end of the table, and at the other the county magnates appeared to be as vehemently cheering their future Member, that a very quiet little man in a black coat, who sat somewhere about the middle of the table, and seemed to take a singularly quiet enjoyment in the scene, found a friendly hand suddenly slap him on the shoulder.

"My dear fellow, I'm delighted to see you! Hope you've enjoyed yourself."

The speaker was the Marquis Mount-Trevor, and with his most smiling, most facetious, most agreeable manner, he held out his hand to the Editor of the *Blankshire Guardian*. The latter had not been able to reconcile himself to refusing a courtesy which had been proffered by a gentleman after conferring on him an essential service. So he had accepted his invitation, and in the same spirit accepted Lord Mount-Trevor's proffered hand and his pleasant advances, to which, of course, he replied in appropriate terms.

His lordship drew a chair near that part of the table, and staid a few minutes gossiping in his most affably facetious mood. He made himself as usual exceedingly pleasant; but on that memorable occasion all the company were similarly influenced.

The Hunt dinner added immensely to Mr. Drelincourt's popularity. He was gratified by finding that his kindly attention to the Editor of the *Blankshire Guardian*, had not been cast away like seed upon a rock. In its next impression appeared an account of the Meet at the Hall without the slightest abuse of its proprietor. It was not a screaming article by any means.

It contained a highly picturesque narrative

of the romantic adventure in which Lady Augusta and Miss Drelincourt had shared, and, much to the satisfaction of the Marquis, there was not so much as the slightest allusion in it to his own adventure which had covered him with mud, and, but for his diplomacy, would have covered him with as much ridicule. There was nothing offensive in the paper; it was in every way creditable to the editor.

CHAPTER VI.

LAYING THE FIRST STONE.

It was a grand day for Middlecombe Regis. That imaginary Methusalem so familiar in English popular topography could not remember so grand a day in the parish. Indeed, individuals of wider territorial memories could not recollect so grand a day in the county. Moreover, the parish clerk and the National School master, each in a new suit of clothes and with a large rosette of true-blue ribbon on the breast of his coat, enthusiastically agreed that there had never been so grand a day in the kingdom.

Every body—gentle and simple—appeared to have got on new clothes, and the number of new hats and smock-frocks among the rural population, would have made an astounding statistical report in the eyes of a Poor Law Commissioner. The children belonging to the schools, in the freshness of their garments, looked as clean and bright and bronzed in their complexions as so many halfpence and penny-pieces of the latest coinage, their juvenile metal rendered more attractive by a profusion of new ribbon and a display of fresh flowers, which every one wore as an addition to his or her particular uniform.

The aged poor of both sexes came out of their cottages into the sunshine, looking almost as spruce and gay as those fabulous specimens of restoration that belonged to an exhibition familiar to the author's youth—people who had been ground young. Wonderful were the metamorphoses apparent in those humble thresholds; not only did the decrepit look overflowing with lusty life, but the paralytic appeared to enjoy the jolliness of robust youth.

More surprising than all was the air of respectability which distinguished a certain portion of the population in whom that sort of thing had never been seen before, even in the smallest possible quantities. The tag-rag and bob-tail of the place had evidently been economizing it all their lives to produce it on this important occasion. The disreputable, the discreditable, the idle, the profligate, and all the infinite variety of rural riff-raff, had washed their hands and faces, combed their irregular heads of hair, renovated shabby wide-awakes, cleaned up dissolute fustian jackets, patched dishonest corduroys, and polished poaching high-lows, in a manner truly miraculous. And they strolled carelessly along the village with a flower in their mouths and a bit of ribbon in their button-holes, looking so wonderfully improved, that the policeman might have been doubtful of their identity.

Even the bandy-legged pot-boy at that notorious beer-shop, "the Bank of England," who had been in the county jail half his life, having put on a bright-sleeved waistcoat, bran-new Bluchers, a clean apron and stockings, and having parted and smoothed his carroty hair and scrubbed his pock-marked face, looked as exemplary, and as estimable a member of society as if he had been qualifying himself for a public appearance at the next demonstration of the Blankshire tea-totallers.

Then the good humour that flourished in every direction! Parties came across the fields from Middlecombe Parvum, groups flocked along the roads and lanes from Middlecombe Magnum, a good many from considerable distances, but all in their holiday suits, and on their best behaviour; and they fraternized with the villagers, and the villagers fraternized with them—men and women, boys and girls, in every imaginable classification of agricultural humanity, displaying uncommon broad grins under head-dresses of the latest rustic fashion, and uttering friendly exclamations and cordial recognitions of the latest social currency.

Much in the same way came horsemen, and men in carts and gigs, farmers and tradesmen, all apparently as jolly as sand-boys, hailing everybody by his Christian name, and that familiarly abbreviated. Then came equestrians of a higher class on better horses, and in smart dog-carts, or dashing buggies, young men got up regardless of expense, generally smoking cigars or meerschaums; intensely amiable to rustic beauty, and profusely liberal of small jokes and coppers to rustic juvenility.

Lastly came the county magnates, riding or driving with rather more than their usual state, and apparently a good deal more than their usual benevolence, for the coachmen and footmen were prodigal in flowers and favours, and their masters and mistresses were as extravagant in smiles and bows, when the rural mind recognized their greatness with the customary noisy compliments. Shouts "rent the skies" when the Marquis Mount-Trevor came on the scene, driving the Marchioness in his handsome phaeton, his lordship, with his stereotyped facial pleasantry, nodding right and left, her ladyship sitting back with her usual serene repose, smiling exquisitely, and bowing inimitably now and then.

Shouts that ought to have done nearly as much damage overhead arose when the Right Reverend Dr. Crumpe's venerable head was seen slightly emerging from the ocean of Lady

Dorothea's flounces that filled the episcopal chariot, which acclamations the good Bishop and the good Bishop's stately wife recognized in their most episcopal manner.

Great cheering arose when an open carriage appeared, bearing those popular county magnates Sir Pouncefort Pouncefort, the Hon. Major-General Toplofty, and Admiral Lord Bluffington, who, in their own peculiar manner, acknowledged their flattering reception. But the skies ought to have suffered dreadfully when a four-in-hand came in sight, the team adorned with flowers and ribbons, driven in grand style by the youthful Sir Charles Forrester, conveying on the drag the Honourable Captain Mildrington, of the Grenadier Guards, Lord Adolphus Fitzpatrick, and at least half-a-dozen other fashionable celebrities, while the inside was crammed with elegant ladies, whose prodigious draperies almost concealed their handsome faces from the public gaze. The shouts were renewed with additional vigour, when, on the panels, large letters became conspicuously visible, making the inscription

"VOTE FOR DRELINCOURT!"

The young and fashionable dragsman and all his young and fashionable companions, acknowledged the cheering by waving their Oxfords, and cheering in return, removing their cigars very amiably for that purpose. Moreover, there was a flutter of lace at the open windows, which proved that the fair insides were of the same way of thinking as their relations and friends on the roof. This seemed exceedingly edifying to the rural mind, for the cheering continued as long as the vehicle was in sight.

Many other carriages entered the village, their occupants receiving similar honours. The pedestrians were getting tired of giving the meed of popularity to all comers, when a hack chaise came in view—very shabby, very dusty, and very disreputable looking, after the stylish vehicles that had passed in such numbers. Seated on the rail in front, to which he held on vigorously with both hands, appeared a remarkably long-legged youth, in a nondescript livery, profusely ornamented with buttons on the breast, and a glazed hat, looking half-throttled by a very stiff white cravat. He stared about him as if as much alarmed as astonished by the signs of popular excitement that met his gaze.

No sooner was his singular figure and remarkable aspect observed, than the cheering broke out more tumultuously than ever, mingled with a good deal of laughing and jocose observations.

A respectable old gentleman's head was thrust out of one of the windows, the florid face bearing evidence of unusual gratification on the part of its owner, and repeatedly made Mandarin movements towards the shouting mob, which seemed greatly to increase their voice. No one had the slightest knowledge of the amiable stranger or of his astonished flunkey; but observing that the former took their cheering as a genuine compliment, and that the latter opened his mouth and eyes wider as the crowd became more noisy, they increased their demonstrations with what was almost a frantic jocularity.

The delighted inmate of the vehicle was Mr. Vitruvius Palladio Crockett, of the eminent firm of Crockett and Finial, architects, of London. He had come by express to the nearest station to reach Middlecombe Regis in time to assist in an exceedingly interesting ceremony, but he had not entertained the most remote conception that his professional reputation was so high in that part of Blankshire.

It was, of course, a grand day at Middlecombe Regis, and he was not surprised at the neighbourhood making the most of it, as it was evidently doing, and to be sure it ought to be considered quite as much a grand day for Mr. Vitruvius Palladio Crockett, but he was not prepared for this hearty acknowledgment of his being its hero. So he maintained his bald head at the window of the post-chaise, smiling blandly, and performing the most expressive genuflexions—even debating in his mind whether he ought to stop the postillion and make a speech.

All the while, the overgrown London page, brought down to swell the dignity of Mr. Vitruvius Palladio Crockett, F.S.A., did not succeed in maintaining his own. He seemed to be miraculously performing a prolonged shake, without any assistance from his vocal powers, and clung to his unpleasant perch, looking like a sickly parrot, who expected to be stoned, and had not the power to fly; for the small editions of Middlecombe Regis humanity, not satisfied with howling at him the most aggravating observations, made believe to rush at a heap of stones in preparation for the macadamized road, as if with the intention of availing themselves of the capital cock-shy he presented. He seemed every minute to be growing stiffer in his new livery and tighter in his white cravat, as he continued to gape in astonishment, and squint from side to side with the most piteous expression of fear and discomfort.

Yes, it was a proud day for Middlecombe Regis, and naturally a very proud day for Mr. Vitruvius Palladio Crockett, of the eminent firm of Crockett and Finial, for it was the day that had been appointed for laying the first stone of the new parish church, parsonage, and schools, and Mr. Vitruvius Palladio Crockett had had the honour of designing these interesting edifices.

It is necessary, however, to the proper appreciation of my story, that the reader should be hurried away from his or her sympathy with that gentleman's extravagant satisfaction, and from his or her commiseration of his most uncomfortable attendant, to the great spectacle of the day, the scene of the memorable ceremony that had attracted all the rank and fashion, gentility, respectability and vagabondism of the county.

A space had been cleared for the foundation, an elevated position in the village selected as the best site which could be procured in the entire parish. This and the most convenient spots adjoining had been reserved for the ladies and gentlemen who were expected, to some extent by themselves, to form the attraction of the glorious spectacle.

In about the most prominent position was seen the Right Reverend Dr. Crumpe, the Lord Bishop of the Diocese, in full canonicals, with several of the neighbouring clergy, among whom the Reverend Septimus Fairholme had found a place. The Bishop was gracious, indeed appeared unusually pleased with him, had praised his zealous performance of his clerical duties as most satisfactorily established by the gratifying reception he, the Bishop, had met with from Mr. Fairholme's parishioners. The zealous Curate looked the intense satisfaction he felt. He was far from being worldly-minded, but the high opinion expressed by his Bishop in the hearing of his brother clergymen gave him very great pleasure.

A little apart from the clerical group, appearedthe well-known figure and face of the Right Honourable the Marquis Mount-Trevor. The Bishop was gracious—mildly, benevolently, gravely gracious; the Marquis was also gracious, but this temporal peer's graciousness was of a totally different type. He was affably, smilingly, jocosely gracious; his superabundant pleasantry, however, on this occasion tempered by a sense of the gravity of the part he was about to play in the eyes of the Blankshire public.

For was not that group of men with note books conveniently placed for hearing and observation, betwixt the wind and his nobility, reporters of the *Blankshire Telegraph* and the *Blankshire Guardian*, and had he not too been told, that artists had been sent by the *Illustrated London News*, and *the Builder*, for the purpose of procuring illustrations of the coming spectacle, and of the intended structure; moreover, had he not just been informed by one of the county magnates, that a certain eminent barrister, who enjoyed the reputation of being 'Our Special Correspondent,' to a certain highly influential London journal, on affairs of unusual public interest, was in that little group, evidently to give an unusually good report of the proceedings. Lastly, could he not see a fellow perched just above him with a camera, absorbed in the occupation of adjusting his machine with the object of providing the Stereoscopic and Photographic Company with a successful negative of that important scene?

It behoved him, therefore, to look as if he felt that he was not Lord Mount-Trevor under ordinary circumstances; he was not to be merely a model patrician Paterfamilias, but a model patrician as well. So, while his lordship was being universally amiable, noticing a consequential personage with a roll of paper in his hand, rather fussily forcing his way through the extremely genteel crowd that surrounded the county magnates, he at once guessed his business, and beckoned him to come forward.

The extremely genteel crowd made way, and the county magnates made way for the stranger, and presently the bald head and well got-up person of Mr. Vitruvius Palladio Crockett, F.S.A., were displaying the owner's studied dignity of deportment, in a series of movements in the direction of the Marquis of Mount-Trevor and the Bishop of Blankshire, which the lay and spiritual peers were content to recognize with somewhat slight and hasty genuflexions.

Then Mr. Vitruvius Palladio Crockett, at an amiable suggestion from the Marquis, unrolled one of the papers he had brought with him, and Lord Mount-Trevor immediately appeared to take in the drawing it displayed the greatest possible interest, and Dr. Crumpe on the other side of the attitudinizing architect immediately appeared to take the greatest possible interest in its details. Then the county magnates who tried to get a peep over the shoulder of their chief, appeared to take the greatest possible interest in the drawing; then the clergy who could see over their little Diocesan were absorbed in the same interest; and the extremely genteel crowd, and the crowd whose gentility was equivocal, and the crowd that had no pretensions to gentility whatever, seemed to be equally interested though they could only see the colour of the drawing paper, and many were prevented from getting even a glimpse at that.

Then the drawing was handed to a group of ladies a little in the rear, which caused a sympathetic flutter in all the female drapery then and there displayed; but the group consisted only of the Marchioness and Lady Theodosia, Miss Drelincourt, Lady Augusta Leigh, and Miss Lætitia Fairholme; and Lady Theodosia having examined it through her gold eye-glass, and delivered herself of a few favourable comments, addressed to the Marchioness, delivered it back into the hands of her lord.

"Bishop!" her ladyship exclaimed, rather loudly for exclusive communication. "The ceremony ought to begin."

At once the drawing was thrust away into the possession of the architect, and at once a description of the remarkable features in the intended structure, which he was in the very act of delivering to the Marquis, was cut short by a general movement of the Diocesan and his clergy, and a general taking off of hats among the male spectators. The Bishop, with impressive solemnity, offered up a prayer, and there was a profound silence while it lasted, then a hymn was sung by the children of the schools, who had been placed a little to the right of the clergymen, most of whom assisted in the singing, in conjunction with several serious young ladies of the neighbourhood.

Then the Marquis Mount-Trevor with a silver trowel in his hand, which had hitherto been concealed, came forward, where a large stone was suspended over a space cleared for the foundation, and commenced a speech. Evidently fully impressed with the gravity of the occasion, as well as with the presence of the reporters, the artists, the special correspondent, and the camera, he made a short oration,—wonderfully short was it for the number of persons he contrived to compliment in it,—for he complimented the Bishop in a manner that elicited tremendous cheering; he complimented the Curate in a manner that must have been very gratifying to his parishioners, for they acknowledged it most cheerfully; he complimented the architect, which only elicited a mild demonstration of applause; but when his lordship paid his tribute of eloquence in acknowledgment of the liberality of the munificent founder, the cheers and waving of hats and handkerchiefs appeared to be universal.

During this demonstration the orator had time to glance at the little group with note-books, the individuals with drawing-boards, and the man with the camera, and saw that they were all as busy as bees in a flower-bed. Then the Mount-Trevor eloquence seemed to gain new vigour, and he complimented the ladies,—and all Blankshire seemed stirred to a man. Lastly, referring to his own humble share in that day's memorable proceedings, his lordship gracefully yet gravely stepped forward, a creaking noise was heard, the noisy plaudits were hushed, and everyone's attention absorbed in watching the descent of the large block of stone.

As it descended to its appointed place, the Marquis first hammered it with the handle of his trowel, then deliberately taking some mortar, handed to him by the builder, plastered its surface as scientifically as if he had been a mason. There was tremendous shouting when the stone was laid, to which the Right Honourable stone-layer responded with an urbanity worthy of a Mount-Trevor performing in public, while he knows that three portraits of him are being taken simultaneously, and every word he utters carefully noted down for general circulation.

When the applause had ceased there was a call for the Bishop, which brought Dr. Crumpe forward again; but it was merely to make a very gracious speech, in which he in turn complimented Lord Mount-Trevor, and then, a little more at length, Mr. Drelincourt.

This gentleman's name was a signal for uproarious cheering, in the midst of which, he, who had hitherto remained quite in the background conversing with Professor Grauwacke, presented himself. The applause increased—Sir Charles Forrester and his young friends making themselves very conspicuous in maintaining it.

When sufficient quiet was restored Mr. Drelincourt made a brief speech, as remarkable for its modesty as for its earnestness of feeling, in reference to the Church, to which it was the speaker's special privilege, he said, to belong.

The Bishop was pleased with it, and publicly shook hands with the orator, in token of his approval. The Bishop's lady was equally pleased with it, but was in doubt whether the act of sociality she had just witnessed was sufficiently episcopal under the circumstances; but then, as she knew too well, the Bishop was always forgetting his eminently sacred position. The clergy were particularly pleased with it, because they saw that their Diocesan was pleased; and the laity were pleased, but, I believe, the majority at least, from purely secular causes.

Now the National Anthem was sung by every one in general and no one in particular—the extremely genteel joining musically with the county magnates here and there; but the equivocals and ultra-nobodies displaying their loyalty with more force and less tune everywhere.

Symptoms appeared of a break-up. There was a general movement of the smartest hats and bonnets of the ladies, as though for an interchange of opinion, followed by a flutter of expansive flounces, and a stir of shawls, mantles, jackets, and Garibaldis of the newest pattern and the most expensive fabric. Some looked at the hands of their gold watches, others examined the fastenings of their cameo brooches and their gold bracelets; the elder young ladies scrutinized the sky, the younger the gentlemen, and all the feminine community seemed to be meditating a change of position.

Nor was the male moiety entirely absorbed in the performance of "God save the Queen." The Bishop had made his way towards Lady Theodosia, and was mildly receiving that august lady's solemn commentary on the un-episcopalness of indiscriminate hand-shaking. The Marquis Mount-Trevor was on his way to the Marchioness, dispensing affability and good-humour among the clergy and laity, right and left. The clergy were on the look-out for serious young ladies, who deserved to be objects of their especial consideration; and the county magnates were comparing notes on the ceremony they had just witnessed, with amazing volubility and animation, as if they considered themselves the only parties having any real concern in it.

The gentlemen of the press had done with their note-books and had put them in their pockets, the artists were finishing their sketches, and the camera was being packed up. Mr. Drelincourt's buff waistcoat and white hat were seen moving forward amongst the gentilities, his handsome head bowing frequently, his fat hand constantly grasping some other hand that was shot forward to meet it, and a considerable amount of pleasant under-talk and bye-play seemed to mark his course, till he came to the gentlemanly-looking eminent barrister already referred to, to whom he said something that was graciously received.

Both gentlemen simultaneously took off their hats, simultaneously shook hands, and chatted with great apparent cordiality for two or three minutes. Then there was another cordial grasp, and the attentive and evidently well-pleased master of "the Hall" proceeded to the gentlemen with the note-books, to the artists, and to the camera—going through much the same process with similar satisfaction to himself and them.

Lastly he made his way back, taking off his hat, bowing, shaking hands, and interchanging short confidential communications, while the vocal part of the spectacle were energetically confounding the politics, and frustrating the knavish tricks of Her Majesty's enemies, in a manner worthy of Blankshire loyalty.

"I suppose this fun is over," observed the Captain of the Grenadier Guards to Lord Adolphus Fitz-Patrick, who was stifling a yawn with his scented pocket-handkerchief.

"Really, now—'pon my honour," replied that exquisite, languidly, "I'm not positively certain, but the thing seems to be dying a natural death. Forrester, my dear fellow," he cried to the young baronet, whose attention seemed absorbed in watching a distant group of ladies, "the Captain wants to know if this dreadful fun is over."

"No!" replied Sir Charles, "not by any manner of means. What we have heard and seen are merely the preliminaries. There is a magnificent *déjeuner à la fourchette* to come off at the Hall, after this affair is at an end; and, thank goodness, it is now on its last legs."

"That's a refreshing idea—isn't it Fitz-Patrick!"

"Really now, 'pon my honour, it absolutely reconciles me to this dreadful thing. Of course the ladies will muster pretty strong?"

"No doubt of that, the dear creatures have come on purpose. Old Drelincourt is a perfect brick, and has invited all the prettiest women within twenty miles."

"How extremely nice!"

"I thought there was a fairish exhibition of that sort of thing. But what's become of the two heroines? I made sure of their being here."

"Miss Drelincourt I saw just now talking earnestly to the parson's sister. Lady Augusta I haven't been able to discover. I hope the poor child hasn't been so seriously damaged as to be obliged to keep her room. No—Yes—there she is, up in that out-of-the-way corner!"

The young men looked earnestly in the required direction.

"She's got her arm in a sling, and looks almost as grave as that old cat of a governess who is talking to her."

"Solemn fact!" exclaimed the Honourable Captain Mildrington, touchingly.

"Really now, I feel quite concerned about her. Awfully concerned, upon my honour. Poor little thing!" added Lord Adolphus, with profound pathos.

The steeple-chasers were, to do them justice, affected by the serious change which was evident in that popular young lady, and indeed so were all the youth of Blankshire, many of whom had come long distances with the hope of being able to effect an introduction to her.

Lady Augusta seemed inclined to treat them with supreme indifference. She neither gave them a look, nor a thought. A change had evidently taken place, or was taking place, in her. She studiously remained as much out of the way of public notice as possible, and when she left the site, disappeared suddenly from view, to the great mortification of her admirers, through a private door in the park palings near which she had been standing, that opened on a walk that led from the Hall to the church—no one accompanying her but Miss Drelincourt and her governess.

CHAPTER VII.

OUT-OF-DOOR RECREATIONS.

The *déjeuner* was a great success. No one in any respect eligible to appear at a fashionable gathering, had been overlooked, and the party consequently was a large as well as a brilliant one. But so excellent were the arrangements that every one could comfortably display his or her social consequence, and the ladies, who mustered in large numbers, enjoyed unheard-of advantages in showing off their toilettes and their amiability.

The large apartments in the Hall had been turned into breakfast-rooms, having tables all along their length and across their breadth. In addition, large and small marquees had been erected in the lawn to accommodate large and small parties. The show of good things, as well as of plate, china, and glass, and the array of domestics in attendance, astonished even the guests who might be thought the least likely to be surprised at such an exhibition.

A more pleasant assemblage had apparently never been brought together. Nothing could be so pleasant to the eye as the harmony of colours produced by the exquisite bonnets, and the charming Garibaldis, cloaks, mantles, shawls, jackets, and skirts—except, of course, the faces and the forms they adorned,—and nothing more pleasant to the ear than the silvery laugh, and gay and sparkling speech of the happy wearers, as they enjoyed the various delicacies, in company with well-looking and well-dressed cavaliers, whose glances, tongue, and hands were equally at their service.

It is impossible to describe the gaiety of that scene — the fashionable ladies generally seated—gentlemen generally standing, and the pleasant confusion of eating, drinking, gossiping, flirting, laughing, joking, going on amongst them at a marvellous rate of progress. Every one appeared inclined to make the most of the occasion for showing the sunny side of his or her disposition, and consequently the general aspect was wonderfully brilliant. Those who were expected to shine in such assemblages, put forth all their social light, as if determined on taking the shine out of everybody else; and those who had never been known to be luminous under any circumstances, put themselves forward as if the brilliancy around them had penetrated the density of their darkness.

The chief charm of the scene was its intense sociality. Provincial gatherings are spoiled by the spirit of exclusiveness that much too frequently prevails in county coteries. Now, this was scarcely at all visible at Mr. Drelincourt's *déjeuner*. The old families joked and laughed with the new, the professional rich were amiable to the commercial rich—and the manufacturers who kept their carriage were sociable with the respectables who were content with a hired conveyance. The popularity of the host seemed to act as an amalgam on the various metals of his numerous admirers, and help them towards a homogeneous composition.

Yet that gentleman by no means put himself forward conspicuously. To be sure he laughed with the laughers, and joked with the jokers—was lively with the young ladies, and courteous to the old ones,—listened to Admiral Lord Bluffington's account of the boarding of the French man-of-war, as if he had not already heard it a dozen times; and with the same respectful attention allowed Lady Dorothea to describe all she had done in behalf of the Patagonian mission, as if he had not already put his name down for a handsome subscription; but he was neither familiar nor servile; neither pushing nor awkward. He felt himself at home in his own house, and was evidently beginning to feel himself at home in the character he had determined to support there, and wherever else it might be necessary for him to play it.

The heiress might perhaps be a little less at her ease, but there were causes that disturbed her equilibrium more than the placid patronage of the Marchioness, or the untiring counsel of the Bishop's lady. She kept as much as she could out of the way of admiration, but being an heiress, the daughter of the most popular man in the county, and moreover a heroine in her own right, it was quite impossible that she should avoid the devotion of the crowd of admirers ready to acknowledge her claims on their attention.

The youth of Blankshire were not to be easily put aside, particularly the steeple-chasers already described, who were impelled towards her by an overpowering sense of their duty to the young lady, and by quite as strong a desire to be favourably known to her. The result was, a constant succession of introductions, and a continual flow of compliments that were rather wearying, and anything but acceptable. She could not help feeling irritated at the prolonged absence of her lover; but this feeling, instead of forwarding the advances of those who would have been only too glad of taking his place, made such approaches less easy.

Sir Charles Forrester sought her acquaintance, confident in the knowledge of his youth, his handsome face, his fine estate, and his baronetcy. He was received kindly, but he owed this to his having been the playmate of her affectionate friend Lady Augusta. The Honourable Captain Mildrington, of the Grenadier Guards, no less confident of his whiskers and his dress, was received kindly, but he owed this to the young lady's knowledge that he had distinguished himself in the Crimea; and Lord Adolphus Fitz-Patrick, equally confident of his personal attractions, and of being the brother of a Duke, was received kindly, but he owed this to a consideration of the political influence of his lordship's family in the county, which she was aware was being exerted in her father's favour.

Each was perfectly content with his reception by the heiress, and founded on it a belief that he was destined to cut out Lord Lionel Leigh in no time. But each was disappointed at not finding Lady Augusta with her—for they had looked forward to making themselves acceptable to two heroines, and felt that they had been defrauded of half their gratification. They found, however, that there was nothing for it but to wait and look about them. Charley Forrester expressed a decided opinion that the tantalizing little chit would be sure to turn up somewhere, and with such consolation his friends were obliged to be content.

It would be unfair to pass over Lord Mount-Trevor, for on the present occasion the Marquis seemed to be intent on excelling himself, so extraordinary were his exertions to be affable and facetious. He smiled, he grimaced, he gossiped, he joked without intermission. He related anecdotes without end.

He was last seen in the centre of a circle of lady admirers describing his wonderful ascent of Monte Rosa, evidently creating quite a sensation.

As the people became satisfied with their refreshment, they left the tables and sauntered into the garden and park, where the juniors amused themselves with playing at croquet and other out-of-door games, and the seniors strolled about the walks, admiring the flowers and the statues, and gossiping to their hearts' content.

Among the earliest who thus employed themselves were a rather striking couple—a venerable little man, in black coat, a shovel hat, and a silk apron—and a graceful girl of fashionable appearance whose right arm was suspended in a sling. They were conversing earnestly and seriously, the silken hair of the one, at the back plaited into a circular knot that the pretty hat upon it did not in the least conceal, bending closely, it might be reverentially, to the close-cut silvery head of the other, almost hid by its ungainly covering.

Even a back view of them sufficed for their recognition. No one could mistake their figures, and the three young men who watched them with the greatest possible animation, from a distance, knew that they were Bishop Crumpe and Lady Augusta Leigh. There was much lively talk amongst this precious trio, but they did not attempt to disturb the privacy of the apparently ill-matched pair. At last—some plan of action perhaps having been arranged—the Baronet turned leisurely into a gravel-walk by himself, and the others proceeded together in a different direction.

"Miss Drelincourt is very good, Bishop," said the young lady, in a grave, earnest voice, "and I should wish to be like her. I don't think I am, though, by a very long chalk."

"Pardon me, Lady Augusta," exclaimed the prelate, in a sonorous though evidently kindly manner, "That last phrase I do not think quite appropriate."

"Ah! that is just what Miss Drelincourt is constantly saying; and I am sure she is right. I try to talk differently to please her, but somehow or other I am constantly saying something I ought not. Yet, Bishop, no one ever complained that I was cheeky."

"There, again," said Dr. Crumpe, more gravely, "that is not at all a proper word for a lady to use."

"What is a fellow to do?" cried his fair companion.

"You really, my dear Lady Augusta, must not consider yourself a fellow. Apparently that is the root of the mischief."

"It's precious hard lines."

The Bishop shook his head. He seemed about to come to the conclusion that the offender was incorrigible. He looked into her fresh, innocent, yet troubled face, and his good heart was filled with pity. How completely that young and lovely creature must have been neglected, he thought, to have imbibed all this bad teaching. Overflowing with Christian charity, he would try another remonstrance.

"Now let me suppose for a moment, Lady Augusta, that you were my own daughter."

"Well, Bishop," she answered, with a doubtful look, apparently not quite appreciating the imaginary position, from the necessity of having the stern Lady Theodosia as a mamma.

"I should then have the inexpressible privilege of remonstrating with you as a parent. My precepts would naturally have more weight with you."

"I don't think you'd make a bad governor. But please to say whatever you like, Bishop. I know you mean me nothing but good, and I shall pay the greatest attention to what you say."

"I feel confident, my dear child," continued the amiable prelate, quite affectionately, "that you are gifted with an excellent disposition, and that if you give your naturally good qualities fair play, there will be no difficulty in your becoming a perfect young lady, as well as an admirable Christian."

"Like Henrietta Drelincourt?"

"Like Miss Drelincourt."

"Oh, wouldn't that be jolly!"

"Lady Augusta!" cried poor Dr. Crumpe.

"Oh, I beg your lordship's pardon!" exclaimed the fair culprit, looking vexed and penitent. "I meant to say, wouldn't that be excellent."

The good Bishop recovered his serenity.

"If I could only be like her! *Per Jupiter!*"

The Bishop looked horrified, and threw up his hands in despair. "Lady Augusta, that is a profane oath, only used by heathens."

"Oh, I'm very sorry. I really did not know there was any harm in it. I will never repeat it, since you say it is wrong. Please to forgive me. I assure you I will try all I can to become like Henrietta Drelincourt. I will now go and look for her, and bring her to you, and your lordship shall see how well I can behave."

The smile on the beautiful young face was so completely that of an uncorrupted heart, that Dr. Crumpe found it impossible to look displeased. As she turned her buoyant figure away, he pursued the path in which they had been rambling, not quite without a hope that he should be able to render the poor child a great and lasting service. She turned down another path leading towards the house, looking a good deal graver than usual. Indeed her happy face was clouded with a painful gravity.

"I've found you at last," cried a well-known voice, "and a precious deal of trouble I have had in looking you up."

"Ah, Charley, is it you?" she replied, with a little confusion, giving her hand into that of Sir Charles Forrester.

"To the best of my belief it is. But you mustn't go yet, Pussy. I'm dreadfully sorry about your arm; all the fellows are sorry, you know. Every one talks of your pluckiness, and I'm proud of my playmate, I am—uncommon proud."

Lady Augusta looked pleased.

"Now I'll bet you a tener to half-a-crown that——"

The remainder of the sentence was delivered in so confidential a tone, that it could not be overheard.

"I shall do nothing of the kind!" answered the young lady, with indignation. "I haven't forgot how shamefully I was sold about the Bishop of Bond Street. I won't take the bet."

"Oh, you're a good deal too good-natured to rip up old grievances," said the young gentleman. "You know what a favourite you always were with me, and how much I have ever admired your——"

"Shut up!" she cried, sharply. "I tell you I won't do it."

"Then I must lose a thousand to Fitz-Patrick."

Lady Augusta had rapidly walked away, with a very determined manner, evidently highly displeased. The last words addressed to her were distinctly heard. She hastened on till she was out of sight of her old playmate, who watched her course with a good deal of serious interest. Then her pace slackened, and her indignation began to subside. Her desire to act properly was very strong, but her affection for Charley Forrester was a good deal stronger. She could not reconcile herself to the poor boy losing such a large sum to that odious

Lord Fitz-Patrick. Still it was clear that she did not like the bet at all. A powerful struggle was going on between her good resolutions and her partiality for her old playmate.

She presently changed her course. She did not take the walk that led to the house, but another that wound round by the lawn. In a few minutes she had rejoined the amiable prelate, whom she found behind a clump of rhododendrons, studying a very strange-looking figure, which apparently he regarded as an African idol.

"It is very curious, Lady Augusta! I wonder if it's Numbo Jumbo?"

"Oh, Bishop, it's nothing of the kind," replied the young lady, evidently with considerable enjoyment. "All the people who come here are expected to fling at it. Unfortunately I can only use my left arm."

She took up a short stick, of which there were several lying about, and hurled it against the uncouth object. It went wide of the mark.

"What an exceedingly singular nose!" exclaimed the Bishop. "Is every one expected to throw at it?"

"Oh yes, Bishop."

"Perhaps to show a becoming indignation at idolatry," he added, quietly taking up one of the short sticks.

Lady Augusta watched him with evident anxiety.

"Every one aims at the head, Bishop."

Dr. Crumpe took a deliberate aim, his fair companion looking on with increasing interest.

Dr. Crumpe flung the short stick, and by some extraordinary luck on the part of the inexperienced flinger, the end lighted on the exceedingly singular nose of the idol, demolishing that feature completely.

There was immediately a subdued laugh from three gentlemen who were looking on at a distance; but more a good deal to Dr. Crump's discomfiture, he heard a voice close to him.

"BISHOP!" it exclaimed, in tones of almost inarticulate horror, "*Playing at Aunt Sally!* How shockingly unepiscopal! Come away this minute."

Lady Dorothea energetically laid hold of the prelate's arm, and her tall figure was presently seen striding along the lawn, carrying her unresisting consort with her.

"You've won it cleverly!" cried the young baronet, coming forward, with his handsome face almost convulsed with laughter.

Lady Augusta took the bank-note offered her, but looked unusually serious for a winner.

"I'm delighted, Lady Augusta, at being able to avail myself of this most agreeable opportunity to a——"

The young lady observed "the odious Lord Fitz-Patrick" eagerly approaching, and knew that more compliments must follow, so with a friendly nod to her old playmate she ran round the rhododendrons, and left the eager steeple-chasers to expend their fine speeches on each other.

It was just as the very agreeable party were about proceeding to their carriages, that Lady Dorothea Scrymgeour, whose stern gaze was fixed upon the Bishop, as he was taking leave of his courteous host, was addressed by a young lady, in a somewhat flurried yet very serious manner.

"Please, Lady Dorothea, to accept my contribution to the Patagonian mission."

"My dear Lady Augusta!" exclaimed that

very dignified personage, as soon as she became aware of the value of the bank-note placed in her hands, " Now I must say that this is exceedingly liberal and thoroughly Christian, and——"

Lady Augusta had disappeared.

From that moment Lady Dorothea took a decided interest in " that dear neglected interesting child."

CHAPTER VIII.

A TEMPLE OF MINERVA.

The school-room at Mount-Trevor Court, like similar places devoted to educational purposes, in other aristocratic mansions, was not a particularly inviting apartment. Perhaps this may have been owing to the necessity of having nothing in it that might divert the attention from the great object supposed to be held in view by its occupants, perhaps to having for several years been in the exclusive possession of boys, who could not be expected to pay much respect to articles of luxury, seeing how roughly they had treated every article of utility in the room.

The Map of the World, hanging on the wall,

had evidently seen a good deal of service as a target for arrows. The books on the shelves appeared to have been mostly employed as missiles for miscellaneous marks, the cracked slates had done duty as battledores and the battered ink-stands as shuttlecocks. The desks and benches seemed to have been employed partly for geographical purposes in tracing the sources of imaginary Nigers, and partly for alphabetical purposes, for the carving of initial letters of an unusual typography.

Over the fire-place was a frame that had once contained a mirror, but in consequence of the brittleness of its material the glass had gone down as suddenly as a barometer before a storm—this indication having been produced one wet day during the holidays by the discharge of a small cannon loaded with slugs. In a niche over the book-shelves there had once been a bust of Dr. Johnson, but the head of that distinguished Lexicographer having accidentally given way under an unexpected shock from his own Dictionary—a shower of Dilworths and Lindley Murrays soon afterwards sent his remains in a vast number of fragments over the floor, which were subsequently used up for chalk drawings and inscriptions in extraordinary variety on every dead wall in the neighbourhood.

On a paralytic chair with one arm, sat the angular form and triangular face of Miss Lucretia Jefferson Stickles, looking more than usually severe out of her sharp grey eyes, as she pored over an open letter, which evidently contained matter of absorbing interest. Opposite, on a superannuated stool on three legs, sat the graceful figure surmounted by the classical head of Lady Augusta Leigh, her bright oval face radiant with the soul's sunshine, as she leaned with both arms over a letter spread on the desk before her.

The hard features of the governess were not only severe, they were anxious in their expression; the countenance of the pupil was not only bright, its brilliance was every now and then tempered with a softness that rendered it still more attractive. The former read on without uttering a word, but her glance seemed to become harder, her lips thinner, and her complexion more sallow as she proceeded—the ejaculations and brief commentaries of the latter were constant. When she did not speak she clapped her hands, and in her eloquent face there seemed a struggle for mastery between tears and blushes.

"O! Miss Stickles, Cass begs his best remembrances to you."

The governess appeared to be as hard of hearing as of features. She could be attentive only to what she was reading. The information was repeated in a more joyous tone. Miss Lucretia seemed to make a powerful effort to divert her attention from the absorbing communication in her tightening grasp.

"O yes! Lord Cassington. His lordship is very good."

She never took her hard look off the paper.

"O! Miss Stickles, he has got quite safe to his destination, and Lionel went with him all the way."

The governess appeared to know that she was not asked a question, for she did not attempt an answer.

"O what fun!" cried the pupil, followed by extravagant clapping of hands.

The governess was mute as death, and her face seemed turning to stone.

A tear now trembled on the long eye-lashes upon the peach-like cheek, while that of her companion seemed every moment to be losing the little humanity that had remained in it. No one could have supposed that such a nature as the one possessed by "the philosophic Miss Stickles," as she had been styled by the *literati* of New York and Boston, could have felt any human weakness; nevertheless, there was not the slightest doubt that she was then enduring quite as much human pain as her philosophy could bear.

But I must give the reader an opportunity of ascertaining the causes of these conflicts of feeling in governess and pupil, by publishing the communication each had received scarcely half an hour before by the foreign post.

"Cincinnatus Jefferson Stickles to his sister Lucretia.

"STICKLESVILLE, May 15th, 186—.

"DEAR SISTER,

"YOURS stating that you had located

among the Britishers came to hand. I guess you're a precious deal too smart for those pudding-headed aristocrats; but then five hundred dollars a year with lodging, board, and washing is a sight more than you could get in the States at teaching; so may be it ain't to be regarded altogether as a bad spec. I reckon you can save out of your fixings a pretty considerable trifle in hard cash, which, at the present price of gold, would pay handsome to invest. I can do a nice thing with it if you send it in coin, as there's nothing so scarce at Washington; but if you'll help me with it for the next contract, I shall be able to make the increase tenfold, as I've got friends at Head-Quarters who assist me in making money that way for a respectable consideration.

"There never were such almighty fine times as these for army contractors—a cute chap can realize a fortune pretty nigh once a week if he ain't too particular. Brown paper can be made to look almost as well as leather, and a good imitation article got up for a few cents as can be charged to Uncle Sam more than as many dollars. If the rebels arn't wiped out too soon I calculate Sticklesville will be a place for you to come back to, as you aren't likely to see in the used-up old country; but the ninety days our President has had to finish them up in, has passed over and over again; that's a fact, and they show more fight than ever.

"All the better for Sticklesville; for more armies must be brought into the field, and more contracts required for stores; and every contract is a precious good haul when the contractor knows what he is about as well as Cincinnatus Jefferson Stickles. I calculate I haven't cleared much less than a hundred thousand dollars by the last. There's nothing like leather, you know, especially when it's made cheap and sold dear.

"Keep the Britishers from supplying the rebels with more Alabamas; we are going to be terribly rampaging about it, and shall wipe them all out of creation as soon as we've exterminated the South. I reckon it's a pity Abe Lincoln don't declare war against them out and out, for there would be another army wanted, and another contract for boots, and I could make another hundred thousand dollars as easy as I could drink a gin-sling.

"There's been a few more battles with losses in killed and wounded as makes Waterloo look contemptible. We can boast of a quarter of a million killed in this war,—a pretty tidy lot for a matter of two years,—the bulk is of course emigrants and rowdies, that are easily spared; but many of the folks hereabouts have never been out of mourning since the first disaster at Bull's Run. Cousins go by dozens, fathers are getting scarce, brothers are thinning out, uncles are scarcely to be had at any price, and male relations generally are rarely to be heard of.

"Brother Tom died at Vicksburg of fever; our cousin Colonel Stickles was killed at Fredericksburg; the Judge was taken prisoner by the rebels, and has not since been heard of; and your uncle General Cassius M. Stickles, who was with the army of the Potomac, was so badly wounded in the last action after the passage of the Rappahannock that he isn't expected to live.

"The rebels have punished us some, that's a fact, and many of our people are beginning to lose heart, and wish the slaughter put an end to; of course they ain't contractors, or they would not be such awful fools. As long as we can get Irish and Germans we can bear any amount of licking, while the Southerners will be gradually wasting themselves away; and such cattle are as plentiful as squashes, so we've only to keep on raising armies, and I have only to go ahead taking contracts, and it's a sure card.

"I think I've nothing more to say except that mother has died of grief, and your aunt Virginia has gone out of her mind, and your cousins have lost all their property in consequence of this war. To tell you the truth, ruin has overtaken many of our best friends, and a good many, not able to stand privations, have died like so many sheep; nevertheless, I don't complain myself; I didn't ought to, seeing that I am doubling my capital almost every month the war lasts.

"And I hope the Confederates may be able to hold out a year or two longer; my place among the Upper Ten will be pretty high, I reckon, if I get a few more contracts between this and then. So keep your spirits up, and don't let any of those pudding-headed aristocrats make you look small. Remember that you belong to the greatest nation on the face of the universal earth, that not only intends to realize the Monroe doctrine, but means to appropriate and annex every bit of worn-out old Europe as soon as we get a chance.

"So hoping to have your remittances by next mail, I remain

"Your affectionate Brother,

"CINCINNATUS JEFFERSON STICKLES."

"P.S.—Awkward circumstances have happened since I wrote the above, which doesn't quite convene at present for me to state in full, for I can't be certain into whose hands this may fall. Let it suffice to know that a large force of rebel cavalry made an unexpected visit to Sticklesville, and what they didn't carry off slick away they burnt to the ground—so that of factory, houses, store, dry goods, furniture, everything,—nothing worth a cent remains. I had news of this as I was liquoring with my friend the Under Secretary at Government House, when he told me that for a certain number of dollars he'd give me valuable information that I should be anxious to turn to profit in less than no time. The dollars, in greenbacks of course, passed like greased lightning from my hand to his, for I knew I could rely on him.

"He drew me aside, and told me that a Commission of Inquiry was then sitting at Washington to investigate the army contracts; that mine was at that moment under consideration, and as the members had found out something not quite satisfactory, a warrant was going to be issued for my apprehension. All I need add is, that I made tracks for Canada, where I arrived safe. I'm in a fix, that's a fact; but if I can hold on amongst the Britishers till this affair has blown over, I don't doubt I shall be able to return to the States in time for another war and another contract."

The other letter was of a somewhat different character.

"Viscount Cassington to his Sister.

"British Embassy, Constantinople,
"May 12th, 186—.

"My darling Pet,

"Here I am as jolly as a fellow can

be, who has gone through such an awful heap of distressing circumstances as have accompanied me ever since I steamed out of Southampton. What I was when I went into the Bay of Biscay, and what I was when I ascended those plaguy stairs at Valetta, it isn't at all in my line to describe. My pen ain't up to making so striking a contrast. The fact is the passage was very stormy. If any advantage is to be gained in diplomacy by my being made to rough it as a preliminary to the study, I think I may claim something handsome that way.

"But it wasn't only the waves and the wind that did it, though I must acknowledge that they spared no exertion to have the roughing all to themselves. By the way, there's just a bare possibility of my having got within an inch of being used up before I turned my back upon town, for I had been suffering from a severe cold and two physicians the week I left, therefore could not be quite in training for going over such a course. So I got awfully punished all the way in such a rough and tumble as was never exhibited in the P. R.

"I got preciously bullied from another source, when too I hadn't so much as the shadow of a chance of doing anything in the way of resistance. Lionel is a tip-top good fellow. It was very brotherly of him to leave such a stunning girl as Miss Drelincourt, to take care of me as far as Malta; and a precious sight of taking care I required, I can tell you. It was still more brotherly of him, when he saw what a helpless animal I had become, to volunteer to see me safe to my destination. But then you see he took advantage of my being down in the world, to pitch into me about my backslidings in so awfully serious a way, that I could find nothing to say for myself.

"I had been a good-for-nothing from my youth upward, and if I did not reflect seriously on my position, I should end in being a disgrace to the family. He gave it me hot and strong, I can tell you. It was rather a bore to be bullied by one's younger brother; but what can a fellow do, prostrate by fever and sickness, and a sense of the truth? I could only cry 'Peccavi!' and I did it lustily.

"Then he went in for another round. And what do you think that was about? Why about you! Solemn fact! He complained of my having spoiled you. He said he had found you unfit for the society of your own sex. He declared that he entertained the greatest fear that you cared only for things that not only were quite unfeminine, but must end in being discreditable. I was knocked down like a shot—doubled up as neatly as a tailor's parcel, and sent into the middle of next week, without a hope of getting back to the day I was living in. So there was nothing for it, but to fling up the sponge, and give in.

"I have promised, therefore, not only to go on better for the future, but to use all my influence to induce you to take an equally new line of country. My darling pet! I really am shocked at finding that I have been doing so much mischief, and as I know what an ace of trumps you are, I should be awfully vexed if you should be looked upon as a low card. I hope therefore that you will try and unlearn everything that horrid wretch Cass has taught you, and be a model of perseverance and industry in the eyes of that singularly strong-minded and strong-featured female, your respected governess, to whom please to present my humble compliments.

"I mean now to enter for the diplomatic stakes, and take up my running, so that when I pass the judge's stand, if I don't come in first I shall second, or else make a respectable third. I won't allow myself to be distanced, if I can help it.

"I am sorry to tell you that the "Arabian Nights" are a dead sell. I have seen nothing in this country that in the slightest degree reminds me of these extremely fabulous tales. Perhaps when I travel eastward, which I mean to do when I can get a chance, I may find myself among the Fatimas, and Aladdins, and Sinbads, honest Viziers, and Commanders of the Faithful, with whom we were so familiar in the pleasant days long gone by.

"I intend to get into harness at the Embassy as soon as possible, and then I have no doubt of being able to pull myself through whatever difficulties may be in my way. I don't say I'll go by everything and everybody, but you shan't be ashamed of my performance on the road of greatness if I can help it. So keep up your good little heart about me. I promise you that I won't be a bit of a Turk to you when I come back, and, moreover, that I won't bring back any Sultanas to put your pretty nose out of joint.

"The City of the Sultan isn't so very bad a place to live in for a change, but you must ask your respected governess about it if you want a description. Kabobs can be made to go down a very hungry man's throat, and sherbet is an innoffensive tipple to the thirsty soul who prefers sweet waters to strong, and pilau may be eaten by any fellow who isn't above sitting down to demolish boiled fowl and rice; but I've found out that better things than these are to be had amongst the true Mussulmans, by an unbelieving dog of a Frank who can pay for a good dinner.

"There's lots of pretty things at the bazaars, embroidered slippers and caps for instance, that wouldn't look badly on a darling pet of a sister that's going to be a stunning good girl; and pretty shawls and scarfs equally likely to find a way into her wardrobe. Be sure, then, to do your best to astonish that not easily astonished governess of yours.

"Nothing will please me more than to be assured that you have turned over quite as new a leaf as I am trying at from my present *trapèze*.

"You will of course send me a few of your pot-hooks by the next mail, with the latest news of everybody and of everybody's wife. Let me know all about the Squire and his improvements, and you and your improvements—in which I assure you I feel a much deeper interest—and how you got on with Miss Drelincourt, and Charley Forrester, and who's married, and who's buried, and who's both, and who's neither. And what's become of all the world, and how the Arab is looking, and how the Bishop; as well as lots of things too numerous to mention.

"Assure Miss Drelincourt that Lionel will return very soon, and tell her to lay the blame of his detention on me. The poor fellow, now he has come so far, must be permitted to see something. I was desirous that he should make a regular tour of it, and do Jerusalem, but he wants to be back to his lady-love, and won't hear of it at any price. Please do the amiable for him with the young lady, for I should be dreadfully put out, if his devotion to me did him any harm in that quarter.

"I don't think I have anything more to say at present, except to urge you to take seriously what I have suggested. My darling pet, I shall be awfully uneasy about you, till I hear that you have given up whatever can be considered objectionable. If you don't get on well with that sublime woman, I shall be obliged to write to the governor in your behalf, for as Lionel says, it's high time your education was properly attended to.

"But I won't bore you any longer with fault-finding, when I can't help seeing that there's more goodness in you than would be found in a dozen young ladies who pretend to be perfection. So let me conclude my darling pet, with the warmest assurances that I am, and ever shall be,

"Your affectionate Brother,

"CASSINGTON."

Lady Augusta had finished the perusal of her communication, had refolded it, and put it in the pocket of her smart apron, when she was a little startled by a suppressed hysteric sob. She turned hastily around, and saw that her companion was under the influence of very strong emotion. Hitherto, there was no one in the wide world whom she so thoroughly detested as this rigid instructress, but her ideas towards her had sensibly softened during the last day or two—that is, since she had begun to take a serious view of her own position; and she had been as careful at her studies as she had previously been the reverse.

Her own feelings had been much affected by the letter she had been reading, but the impression had been pleasurable. A glance told her that her governess had received ill news.

"I hope no misfortune has happened to you, or any of your friends, Miss Stickles?" observed her pupil, kindly.

"No, Lady Augusta, nothing of the sort!" replied the governess, in a sharp tone, making a strong effort to recover her composure, as she locked up her epistle in her work-box.

"This horrid war!" exclaimed the young

lady, still with genuine sympathy. "I was afraid some new disaster had occurred, by which your friends in the North had suffered severely."

"The Federals haven't met with any disaster as I know of," she added, with an expression of mingled scorn and bitterness. "They'll soon be able to whip the rebels right off the face of the earth, I reckon, and will be ready to dispose as effectually of as many more enemies as choose to take part with them."

Lady Augusta could see that she spoke under strong irritation, and prudently said no more. She returned to her lessons, but a message from the Marchioness presently took her out of the room.

She had not been gone many minutes when one of the footmen announced a visitor to the governess, and then a man entered the schoolroom with a brisk step and a quick eye, dressed in a shabby suit of black, with a hat in his hand that appeared to be older even than his clothes. He had rather a dusty face and a very dusty shirt, with an uncommonly high collar.

He came in with a mysterious air, and without saying a word, sat himself down near the governess on a battered chair, looking inquiringly into her face.

"Your name is Stickles?" he said at last.

"I don't want to know that," she answered sharply.

"Of course not, but I could tell you something you *do* want to know," he observed, meaningly.

"I'm not so sure that you can."

"We'll see. You know a place in the Northern States of the American Union, called Sticklesville?"

"It's where I was raised."

"Just so. Do you remember an Englishman visiting in that neighbourhood some fifteen years ago, who called himself the Honourable Sylvester Harcourt—apparently a man of family and fortune—making a tour in the States?"

Hitherto Miss Stickles had treated the questions of the stranger with supreme indifference. The last made her turn deadly pale.

"What do you want asking about that man?" she inquired, fiercely.

"I am a London solicitor, and it is in my power to render you an important service; in fact, I have come here on that errand."

The governess laughed bitterly, with a face almost convulsed with passion.

"Can you tell me if that man is alive or dead?" she demanded.

"He is alive, to my certain knowledge."

She started up with a frantic look, and seized him by the arm.

"Do you know where he can be found?" she asked, hissing the words through her teeth.

"Perfectly."

"Tell me then without a minute's delay—I must see him instantly—I will hunt him through the world—I will——"

"Pardon me Madam, for interrupting you but let me suggest caution and preparation."

"I am quite prepared,—I want only to know where he is."

"Are you in a condition to prove your marriage?" he whispered.

"I have preserved all the documents, and can produce them at any time."

"And I have ascertained the name of the

clergyman by whom you were married,—who happens to be now in this country, and willing to come forward when required."

This also was uttered in a low voice.

"Tell me where he is then!"

"Listen to me. You will be ready at twelve o'clock the day after to-morrow, to place yourself at my disposal. By that time all my arrangements will be completed for taking you to the place where he is concealed."

The excitement of the governess was extreme. The short conference with this strange man, had effected a most startling change in her appearance. From the rigid methodical teacher absorbed in rules, and devoted to study, she had become a passionately vindictive woman, restless under the influence of an eager desire for vengeance.

She pleaded hard for immediate action, but the lawyer was not to be driven a hair's breadth out of his course. He shook his head.

"Caution, my dear Madam, caution. If we are precipitate, we shall lose all the advantages I intend you to obtain. Your husband is not a person to be approached in an ordinary way."

"My husband!" she muttered, clenching her hands, her grey eyes apparently flashing fire.

"My professional reputation, too, is not to be lightly risked—for I am in a manner responsible for his capture."

"Who are you, and by whom are you employed?" she demanded, turning round upon him in her impatient strides up and down the room as he rose cautiously from his insecure seat, rubbing his almost napless hat with his equally napless sleeve, evidently about to take his departure.

"The name of my client prudential reasons induce me to withhold, but here is my card. I particularly recommend you to absolute silence on this confidential business, till I call for you at the time appointed. It is of the utmost importance to the interests of my client, that no suspicions should be excited of my errand, or of your connection with it. I wish you good morning."

When the man had left the room, Miss Stickles glanced at the engraved card of address he had placed in her hand. It bore the inscription :—

MR. PRODD,

ATTORNEY-AT-LAW,

THAVIES INN.

CHAPTER IX.

A TELEGRAM.

The manager's widow stood alone in the parlour of her respectable house in the byè-street of Belgravia, already sufficiently described. The room bore a less littered appearance than usual. There was no cheap material spread on the table; there were no homely-looking garments flung upon the chairs; there were no multifarious odds and ends scattered over the carpet. The official duties of the honorary secretary appeared to be in abeyance, and the honorary secretary no longer in her place.

But if the daughter was absent, the mother was not, and Mrs. Bootles was not a person to be overlooked in her own house. She was there, in the identical parlour, so familiar to the clergymen of the district to whom the privilege of the latch-key had been accorded. What she was doing there, did not very clearly appear.

She was walking up and down the room, but apparently not for exercise. Middle-aged females taking a constitutional—indoors or out—rarely slap their foreheads, and show as much of the whites of their eyes as that Belgravian matron was doing. Some of them, too, though they may study their own dignity in the swell of their crinolines, seldom do so in strides so exceedingly majestic as those which were crossing and re-crossing that particular Brussels carpet. Nor do they usually mutter words of dreadful import as they pass along, in the very emphatic style of declaration employed by Mrs. Bootles.

The walk, the talk, the look; in short, the entire manner of that respectable lady—at the time to which I refer—was exceedingly suggestive of theatrical study. Had the manager's widow voluntarily returned to that brilliant sphere of which she had so long been the chief ornament? Was she preparing for her re-appearance in some of her favourite characters, by particular desire, and for a few nights only?

I am not in a position to answer these questions with a degree of certainty that would satisfy the reader. All I know is that her proceedings were of such a peculiarly marked a nature that no old playgoer observing them could avoid receiving the impression that the legitimate drama, as far at least as the principal female characters were concerned, was then in a state of indiscriminate reference. One moment you seemed to see Katherine in "The Taming of the Shrew," another the equally indignant Desdemonda in "Othello,"—presently there was as distinct a recollection of Milwood in "George Barnwell," which was only obliterated in favour of one equally striking of Margaret of Anjou in "King Henry the Sixth."

The orator's celebrated advice, "Action! action! action!" seemed superseded for that of "Attitude! attitude! attitude!" out of respect for which the manager's widow changed from "grave to gay; from "lively to severe," with a facility rare even in those who effect rapid transformations of character at about the average of fifty for a shilling.

Presently a double knock at the street door caused her to stop and listen, with an intensity of expression worthy only of Morgiana, intent on the destruction of "The Forty Thieves." Then she would recognize the shuffling step of the slip-shod maid on the kitchen stairs and along the passage oil-cloth, the opening of the door, and the voice of a gentleman making an inquiry, and her sternness of look was that of Meg Merrilles in "Guy Mannering."

Anon she heard footsteps ascending to the drawing room, and the door of that highly-respectable first floor open and close, and she turned away and resumed her walk with an injured look, appealing to the ornament in the centre of the ceiling in a way that would have become Lady Douglas, imploring the help of Heaven, before her excellent son Norval comes to her assistance.

Again she strode up and down, very much as if proceeding at the measured step from one wing to the other; again she slapped her forehead, again she wrung her hands, again she shook her head, and again she put her finger to her lip, and paused.

There was a ring at the area bell. She listened.

It was only the milk.

She resumed her stride. She put her index finger of her right hand in the palm of her left, and seemed to reflect.

A loud single knock started her out of that attitude, and she again listened,—this time stooping, with one hand open behind her ear, the better to catch the sound. She uttered an impatient "Psha!"

It was only a hawker.

She drew herself up to the full display of her theatrical figure, and resumed her histrionic promenade. Her pace, however, was slower, somewhat funereal in its dignity; very much in the style of an outraged Virginia going to be immolated by her dreadfully affectionate father. She sunk slowly upon a chair, and rested her head in a very touching manner upon her hand.

A terribly loud postman's knock very

nearly sent her off her equilibrium. With her hand upon the region of her heart, and with the look of a tragedy heroine who has received a mortal stab, she hastily regained her legs. The listening attitude was resumed, till she heard the name announced by the postman. Then she spasmodically clapped her hands together, and with a glance of almost supernatural intelligence, said in a stage whisper—" I thought so."

She walked again briskly, her face very animated in its expression, till she recognized the sound of the latch-key, when she stood still in an attitude of expectation. In a very few minutes the parlour door was pushed open, and Miss Bootles rushed in pale and breathless.

" O mamma!" exclaimed the young lady in a whisper, sinking on the sofa.

" What have you discovered?" demanded Mrs. Bootles in a hoarse voice, but retaining her position on the Brussels carpet.

" O mamma! they wouldn't let me look at the address on the letter that had been posted."

" Shameful!" cried the indignant matron.

"They said I must have the permission of the Secretary to the Post Office."

"Impudent creatures!"

"They declared that a letter once in the box became the property of the Postmaster General."

"Insolent wretches!"

"So mamma, seeing there was really nothing to be done in that way, I left the place, very indignant, as you may suppose."

"Of course, my dear. I know how hard it is to endure the insolence of office, especially from a shop-keeper who ought to be civil. But I shall take my custom away. His 'highly recommended Mixture,' isn't drinkable, my dear, and his 'genuine Mocha' is half chicory.

"Yes, mamma."

"Proceed, Clarissa. You were saying——"

"As I left the shop, I noticed the Reverend Emanuel Mordecate walking hurriedly along."

"Yes, dear."

"And knowing that he had been sent for, and that I had absolutely seen him with my own eyes enter the drawing-room door, evidently with something more than ordinary on his mind——"

"Yes, dear."

"I followed him, mamma."

"You did right, Clarissa."

"I watched him, mamma.'

"You did very right, Clarissa."

"I saw him enter the Electric Telegraph Station."

"Ha!"

At every sentence that had been uttered by Miss Bootles, Mrs. Bootles had advanced a step, and they now stood close together, looking at each other with faces expressing the most profound sense of mystery.

"Well, dear?"

"That's all, mamma. I hadn't waited long before he came out, and I watched him back to our own door."

"It's very strange!" exclaimed the Manager's widow, her head on one side, pondering on the small fragment of information she had received.

"I believe that he is telegraphing at her request."

"There cannot be the slightest doubt of it, Clarissa."

"I should very much like to know what the message was."

"So should I, my dear."

"But as I couldn't ask *her* to tell me—I am afraid to ask *him*—and am certain that if I inquired at the Telegraph place, they would be as uncivil as at the Post Office. I don't see how it's to be ascertained."

"Nor I either, my dear."

"Then there's the strange gentleman, mamma."

"The *uncle*, Clarissa. *Captain* Mauleverer."

Mrs. Bootle's countenance was as significant as her emphasis.

"I don't know what to make of him at all."

"If he's a foreigner he speaks very good English,—much better than Count——"

"Don't mention that horrible wretch, mamma."

"Very well, my dear. But about this imaginary relative speaking English—what were you going to say?"

"I was going to say, mamma, that if he is an Englishman, he speaks very good Italian."

"How do you know, Clarissa?"

"Because I heard him conversing with a man playing a barrel-organ, and he seemed as familiar with that language as the other."

"A good many persons know two languages; indeed, most of the couriers employed by English travellers are acquainted, I have been told, with three or four, so I cannot draw any safe conclusions from that convenient uncle speaking both Italian and English. All I know is, that his coming here is extremely equivocal; and that the coming here of the various gentlemen he brings with him (from the White Horse Cellar, perhaps,) is more equivocal still."

The manager's widow uttered the words in parenthesis, as an aside of unusual significance.

"Then, mamma, hadn't you better give her warning, at once?"

"She pays three guineas a week, Cassandra," she replied, in a stage whisper. "I'm not exactly a fool, my dear."

"No, mamma, certainly, but——"

"It's quite a salary, my dear, when it's regularly paid; and there are neither fines nor stoppages at the treasury."

"Yes, mamma, but——"

"After all he may be her uncle, you know,—this mysterious rich relative, this *Captain*, who is so young looking for an elderly man, and frequents the White Horse Cellar, Piccadilly."

The highly dramatic manner in which the concluding portion of the last sentence was delivered, belonged to the best school of genteel comedy.

Miss Bootles seemed a little perplexed.

"Hush! there is the drawing-room door opening," exclaimed the matron.

"It is Mr. Mordecate going out," added the spinster.

"Shall I follow him again?"

"Yes, but do not let him see that you are watching him. Of course I am most anxious to know the truth, but I could not think of doing anything that might offend a good lodger."

Hardly had the street door closed upon the reverend gentleman, when it was softly opened again. A female stood on the threshold watching his retreating figure. When he had turned the corner, she also closed the door and hurried in the same direction.

Mrs. Bootles was left to resume her solitary promenade and sock and buskin recollections, but as the reader may be considered to have had sufficient of these, he must allow himself to be transported to the floor above, that he may be able to know something reliable concerning the mysterious goings on in the drawing-room.

Everything in that respectable apartment looked very much as it had looked when last described. The lodger, too, was very nearly in the same state as when last seen. The only perceptible difference was, that her face expressed a good deal less of pain and sorrow.

She was engaged upon some fancy work, apparently quite contented if not perfectly happy; but she was not alone. Seated in the best easy chair, was the figure of a gentleman—at least it might be presumed that the entire individual was there, though the only portion distinctly visible comprised a pair of stout legs, encased in stout cloth trousers and shining leather leggings, that came up nearly to the knee, and joined a pair of stout laced boots; the rest of the individual being concealed behind a broad sheet of the *Times* newspaper.

There was certainly nothing very remarkable in what was going on between the ambiguous young lady in Mrs. Bootles' highly-respectable first floor, and the mysterious gentleman from the White Horse Cellar, Piccadilly; the one was innocently threading her needle, and the other was quite as innocently reading a leader on the American war. The worker did not attempt to interrupt the reader, nor the reader the worker. The cleverest detective could have made nothing out of the situation. It was very domestic, but that was all.

Presently the newspaper was folded down to less than half its previous dimensions, and then a dark round face with beard and hair almost entirely black, was seen above it. The complexion was dark enough for a foreigner, so was the hair and thick short beard and moustache, but there was a peculiar expression in the clear eyes that betrayed the John Bull.

Notwithstanding all Mrs. Bootles' doubts and insinuations, the gentleman was no other than Captain Mauleverer, who had left his vineyard in Italy, for the very legitimate purpose of visiting his native country, that he might see justice done to his niece. Very naturally, he spent a good deal of his time in her society, and not unfrequently he had brought old friends to see her, or persons recommended to him as likely to do her service.

Very naturally, his young kinswoman insisted on his resting in Mrs. Bootles' best easy chair, permitted him to stretch his stout legs comfortably over Mrs. Bootles' bright-patterned rug, and provided him with what she knew he would consider the greatest luxury he could enjoy during his stay in England. The consequence was that she worked on and he read on, both perfectly at their ease, without entertaining the slightest suspicion of the feminine volcano beneath them.

Occasionally the young lady, from her lowly seat, directed an earnest glance towards the gentleman in the easy chair, but whether he was eclipsed by the broad sheet, or his well-bronzed good-humoured face shone like a beaming sun above it, she seemed equally content. There was her protector, and her refuge, and she felt secure.

The broad-backed, strong-limbed, "convenient uncle," associated so mysteriously in Mrs. Bootles' highly dramatic ideas with the White Horse Cellar, now and then stole an anxious look over the leading article towards the fair occupant of the ottoman, bending over her work, and having satisfied himself that her troubles had not very severely affected her health, he returned to his reading; but not before he had doubled up his big fist in a way that indicated a hostile state of mind towards somebody.

"Mordecate is either very long, or else I am getting impatient," observed Captain Mauleverer, as he turned his paper.

"He is sure to return as soon as he can, uncle," replied his fair kinswoman, who, however, quite as much felt the delay complained of, as he could have done. She had been listening attentively as she worked, apparently in expectation of some sound.

"Does he know Lord Vallance?"

"I am not certain. He may have met him in Italy."

"I wish *I* had."

The young lady did not immediately reply to that pithy remark, and her stout kinsman having again suggestively doubled up his fist, was once more eclipsed by his newspaper.

"That Father Dermott is a droll fish," he added presently, as his features reappeared above the horizon of type.

"He seems to have seen much of the world, and taken his experience very pleasantly," remarked his niece.

"I've met some good fellows among the Italian priests; but this reverend Irishman deserves to belong to the order of the Jolly Dogs, rather than to the one of which he calls himself the Superior."

"He has been extremely zealous in my service, uncle."

"So he has, my dear. I think the best acknowledgment I can make, will be to send a pipe of wine to his convent; but if the Brotherhood are at all like their Superior, it won't last them long."

Again there was no reply. Father Dermott had dined with Captain Mauleverer the previous day, but the young lady on the ottoman did not think it necessary to inquire the extent of her reverend friend's potations. Whatever may have been the quantity, they had not done him any harm, as she could testify, the good father having called upon her that morning, unquestionably in full possession of his health and faculties.

The uncle retired behind his paper, and the niece divided her attention between her work and the sounds in the street—the latter getting the preference more and more. She appeared now to look anxious and to feel impatient. She knew that a crisis in her fate was impending, and began to grow uneasy as she felt its approach. The future was uncertain, an accident might disarrange all the plans that had been so skilfully laid for her benefit, and she might fail in her object, just when success seemed in her grasp.

A glance more anxious than her own was watching her, and seemed to note the change that was expressed in her features, with growing concern. Captain Mauleverer became more impatient. He turned the broad sheet over and over, without dwelling upon any of its columns, and directed his observation quite as much to the face beyond as to the print before him.

"I wish *I* had gone," he said, hurriedly. "I think I can rely on Mordecate, for I did him a good service, and he hasn't forgot it; but in affairs of consequence one's best friend is always oneself."

"I think I hear him coming, uncle," said his companion, springing up hurriedly, her face considerably paler, and her look and manner betraying no ordinary excitement. A loud knock was heard at the door, and a minute after Mr. Mordecate entered the drawing-room with a paper in his hand.

"Here is the telegram," he said.

Mr. Mauleverer jumped up from his nearly recumbent position, and snatched at it impatiently. He tore it open and read it.

"Hurrah!" he cried, waving it over his head, his brown face looking a good many shades warmer in tint. "We must prepare for a change of quarters."

He handed the slip of printed paper to his agitated niece, who stood beside him supporting herself by a chair. She read the writing upon it; it ran thus:—

"*All right. The thing has been made as safe as the Bank of England. Join me with as little delay as possible.*"

CHAPTER X.

THE COUNTY ELECTION.

It must have rained true-blue ribbon to account for the abundance of this material worn in the most public way in Pudborough, the county-town of Blankshire, and in all the roads leading thereto. Not only must it have rained such ornaments, but there must have been a regular St. Swithin's to have furnished it in such a marvellous quantity.

It was quite astonishing to notice its prevalence in the streets. In the better class of voters, proceeding into the town in carriages or on horseback, gay rosettes adorned the horses' heads and the gentlemen's coats, while the ladies rivalled each other in the ingenious way they had pressed the material into decorative service.

It was much the same with the middle-class voters. Not only the horses, but the vehicles were profusely adorned with streamers and laurel leaves. Manufacturers, professional men, farmers, and tradesmen, generally with their families, were riding or driving into Pudborough as into a fair, in quite a holiday cavalcade, in their best dresses made brilliant with ribbons and flowers.

As for the pedestrians—many of whom had no vote—nothing could be more gay than the appearance of their caps, jackets, and smock-frocks, as they trudged along the roads, except their jovial faces and their jocose exclamations. Everything was true-blue. Broad slips or narrow slips of ribbon were round everything; bows, large or small, were everywhere. The drivers had the party-badge streaming from their whips; and wide-awakes, billy-cocks, Oxfords, and all other varieties of the rural hat, were distinguished in the same gala profusion.

A large body of stalwart miners, looking not unlike navvies in their Sunday apparel, came in caravans, with wives and children, from the works at Middlecombe Regis, not only with true-blue flags and banners waving over their vehicles, which were canopied by bowers of laurel-flowers and ribbons, but with flowers and favours wherever space could be found for them. It flourished in the manes and tails of the heavy cart-horses, as much as in sashes and bonnet-ribbons. The men had even gone to the extragavance of tying their corderoys or moleskins under the knee with the same distinguishing decoration, leaving a streamer on each side the leg.

The thoroughfares not only resounded with continual cheers, but with constant music of some kind or other. Brass bands accompanied large bodies of tenantry; and very few of the groups of agricultural labourers or mechanics belonging to local clubs, but were preceded by an equally noisy vanguard. Those who could not procure regular musicians were content with amateurs on whistle-pipes, banjos, accordions, jew's-harps, and bones; and when instruments of any kind were not to be obtained, had recourse to their "native wood notes wild," in choruses of wonderful patriotic or social fervour.

Even some of the carriages of the county magnates were seen profusely decorated with flags and favours and supplied with musicians, the flunkeys and grooms with immense bouquets and rosettes, having volunteered to distinguish themselves on the occasion by performances on mouth-organs and key-bugles of certain popular tunes, which they had never before attempted out of the servants' hall or the stable.

These spasmodic polkas and consumptive schottisches were immensely cheered; and by the humbler wayfarers, as well as by the inmates of the houses passed on the road, they were received with encouraging shouts and waving of hats and handkerchiefs.

But the most cordial demonstration of this kind was given when Sir Charles Forrester drove by in his gay drag a thousand times gayer than ever, with banners and streamers, and flowers and laurel branches, scattered profusely over horses and vehicle, with Lord Adolphus Fitzpatrick in a conspicuous situation on the roof, playing the cornet-à-piston in a style that would have secured his lordship an excellent engagement at Cremorne.

The principal streets in Pudborough were as lively as the roads leading to that important town. For it should be remembered that it was an ancient city, containing the ruins of a castle that had been fought over by three generations of antiquaries in consequence of its claims to be Roman, to be Saxon, and to be Norman. It possessed a Bishop's Palace, and a union, cavalry barracks, and a manufactory of thimbles; horticultural gardens and a hospital for the blind; an assize court and a mechanics' institute; a prison and a cathedral; with churches, chapels, emporiums, tabernacles, hotels, Bethesdas, and beer-shops in as great variety and abundance as in any country town of its population in the kingdom.

There was a good deal of bustle going on in the place during the assizes, or on a market day, but on an election Pudborough was scarcely to be recognized. That respectable hotel, "The Rose and Crown," situated so conveniently in the market-place was, as usual, the centre of attraction. It had most judiciously been selected as the head-quarters of Mr. Drelincourt's committee, and its entire frontage was adorned with placards, with the usual electioneering announcements and professions, wherever space could be found among the leaves, the flowers, and the ribbons that almost concealed the brickwork.

Banners projected from long flag-staffs; from the first floor Union Jacks; "Vote for Drelincourt," "Drelincourt and Social Progress," and the like, while at the open windows stood several of the leading personages in Pudborough, scanning with considerable interest the stream of people coming in various directions, but all congregating within view of a newly-built timber erection, covered with placards similar to those on the hotel.

This was the hustings—the place where the candidates for the representation of the county were formally introduced to their anticipated constituents, expressed their political opinions, and received the customary cheers and cabbage stumps of the electors. For it was rare indeed that Blankshire had been unanimous in its demonstrations. Time out of mind there had been a popular candidate and an unpopular candidate, and those who had not come to applaud had conscientiously remained to pelt.

Mr. Drelincourt had not been idle. Almost as soon as his influential friends had declared him a candidate, he had commenced his canvass, and with the assistance of his supporters, had made himself personally known to a considerable portion of the constituencies. His progress had been very encouraging; his committee were in high spirits, and he himself not dissatisfied.

Still there was considerable cause for uneasiness. The opposite party were known to be very powerful, but no one seemed to be aware of what they were doing. It was said that a candidate was to be brought forward so very desirable in every way that he was certain of carrying his election; but no one had heard of his name.

Mysterious announcements appeared on all the dead walls of the county, suggesting to the free and enlightened electors of Blankshire the propriety of not allowing themselves to be disposed of by an oligarchy in favour of a nobody; but to reserve their promises till the day of nomination, when a candidate worthy to represent their important county would be made known to them, and would solicit their suffrages. Much speculation ensued respecting this personage; but his name was not suffered to transpire.

It was now the day of nomination, when an end must be put to the mystification, and great excitement prevailed. Obscure hints and dark threats had been freely circulated by "the Pinks," the opposition party who had always been so designated from the colour of their badges; and as the friends of the popular candidate were mustering to his support, evidently in no disposition to suffer affront, it was expected that a collision would take place that might end in a riot, equal in violence to anything of the kind that had occurred at Pudborough in the memory of man. As precautions, additional constabulary were brought into the town, and the soldiers though removed from the barracks were kept under arms at a convenient distance.

A feverish uneasiness prevailed amongst the respectable townsmen and county authorities, particularly when it had been discovered that all the dead cats had disappeared, while the value of rotten eggs had increased at least a penny a score. Every magistrate knew what that meant.

The joyous bands who flocked towards the market-place near the hour of meeting, shouting "Drelincourt for Ever!" although to all appearance very good-humoured fellows, by a certain handy way in which they flourished their stout walking-sticks, seemed not indisposed to use them as weapons upon sufficient provocation. However, no one seemed inclined to molest them. A little electioneering "chaff" now and then was addressed to them as they entered the town; but this they took as a matter of course, returning it with interest. They found before the hustings a compact mass of spectators, the bulk of which were evidently not of their party; nevertheless, the sturdy fellows, whether mechanics, labourers, or miners, generally pushed on and contrived to secure convenient places for seeing and hearing.

The time for commencing the proceedings had arrived, and from the front rank of the little crowd of gentlemen upon the hustings, consisting of the High Sheriff of the county, the principal county magnates, and the popular candidate, with his proposer and seconder, stepped to the front, hat in hand, with the official whose duty it was to open the proceedings. Partly in consequence of the great noise made by the mob, and partly in consequence of the little made by himself, he did not appear to be heard by any one save the reporters, who were observed on the platform diligently taking notes of his speech.

The High Sheriff, though in full costume, was not in full oratory, and the recommendations that were so boisterously flung at him to "Speak up!" did not render the old gentleman's mumble more intelligible to the restless community beneath. However, they cheered him when he came forward, and more lustily still when he retired.

The appearance of Sir Pouncefort Pouncefort seemed the signal for the breaking forth of a most confused medley of sounds. He bowed, for there was a good deal of cheering; he stood upright, with his hand in the breast-pocket of his white waistcoat, for there was a liberal amount of cat-calls, hisses, groans, and bad jokes, mingled with cordial recommendations to "Go to Bath," and polite suggestions to "Cut it short." He was well seasoned to this treatment, and waited, hat in hand, without betraying the slightest impatience, till it was over.

Then in a clear sonorous voice, and in sentences equally familiar to his audience, he proposed John Drelincourt, Esq., of "The Hall," Middlecombe Regis, as a fit and proper representative of the county; dwelling in the usual way on his peculiar recommendations for the distinction, and suggesting, with his accustomed eloquence, the advantages the constituency would receive by selecting him as their member. Then he referred to the patriotism of the party by whom that respectable candidate was supported, and to the good they had invariably done throughout the length and breadth of Blankshire.

He was proceeding to dilate in still more emphatic terms, on the shortcomings of a certain faction that had been always trying to ride over the county roughshod, when his oratory received such a loud and prolonged interruption that he thought it most prudent to bring his proposal to a close.

The Honourable Major-General Toplofty now marched to the front, drew up his military figure, took off his hat, and made his military bow. The noisy honours which had attended the exit of his colleague, with an astonishing access of vigour, were renewed at his appearance. Contradictory shouts assailed him on all sides. He was desired to "mizzle," he was directed to "go ahead." Enigmatical phrases were poured upon him from every quarter, with inquiries equally perplexing. But he stood firm as a rock. He had gone through the ordeal more than once, and, as long as no heavier missiles were used, was willing to endure it again.

The endeavours of his friends prevailed, or the exertions of his enemies abated, for in a few minutes he was permitted to second the proposed candidate in the customary form. But when he went on to denounce the mysterious proceedings of the "Pinks," as more worthy of the Spanish Inquisition than of Englishmen, the cheers and counter-cheers, the shouts and counter-shouts, the praise, the abuse, the commendation and indignation of the opposing forces burst out with such fury that he and the reporters were obliged to stop.

General Toplofty, however, was not to be

driven from his entrenchments ; to say no more than the truth, he rather liked the disturbance he had created, and smiled grimly as he regarded the noisy, restless mass heaving backwards and forwards below. Presently the uproar gradually died away, and he proceeded—

"We have been threatened with opposition, gentlemen," he exclaimed, as soon as he thought he could obtain a hearing. "But in what shape no one is wise enough to say. The 'True Blues' have brought forward their candidate like men, in the open day; all they have done has been above board, their intentions being too honest to require the aid of mystification. They have a battle to fight, and they come forward to fight it manfully—but the enemy, gentlemen, skulks in the dark—conceals his force in holes and corners, and won't show a front anywhere where he could be met in fair fight."

The latter portion of the General's speech was heard in rather a fragmentary state from the frequency of the interruptions;—yells, groans, hisses replied to by vociferous applause, following the delivery of almost every line. At the conclusion, the confusion seemed to reach a climax that rendered any more provocation too hazardous to be attempted, and the seconder, perfectly satisfied with the effect he had produced, prudently retired to the back-ground.

There were indications of active hostilities having commenced in several places, but as soon as the candidate thus proposed and seconded appeared in front of the hustings, the storm seemed to lull as if by magic.

It had been anticipated that on Mr. Drelincourt presenting himself, a general attack would be made upon him by the irritated opposition, which must inevitably be the commencement of a formidable riot, but whether it was from a feeling of curiosity to see an individual respecting whom such strange stories had been circulated, or from the interest many of the crowd must have felt in a self-made man,—who they were well aware, was making a good use of his wealth, —their irritation subsided as soon as they observed the carefully got up country gentleman taking off his white hat, and with his cheerful prepossessing countenance, advance to address them.

They evidently liked his appearance, for they gave him a cheer that seemed both hearty and general, and when he commenced speaking, they listened with every outward mark of attention. They appeared to acknowledge to themselves that the candidate looked both friendly and sincere; and when he began to speak they were soon equally ready to admit that he spoke as if he were in earnest.

He entered into a general exposition of his opinions on the questions of most public interest in Blankshire, avoiding any expression that could be regarded as irritating to the "Pinks," and so shaping his ideas that many who came there as his opponents, began to experience a conviction that he was expressing their own peculiar sentiments. He therefore received a good deal of cheering.

Having felt his way a little into their confidence he commenced more at large to enter upon subjects with which he was thoroughly acquainted—and his audience were not—the proper policy of the country for the full development of the elements of the national prosperity, at home and abroad, when he furnished them with a view of our manufactures and commerce which seemed to astonish as much as it pleased them. He showed them clearly what they really wanted to realize—that advancement in social progress which was essential to their welfare, and having made every voter and non-voter understand that he should enter Parliament with no other purpose than to forward the real interests of that particular individual, his village, his town, his county and his nation, he closed his most successful speech with the Parliamentary candidate's usual hope of being placed at the head of the poll.

When the immense cheering which followed Mr. Drelincourt as he turned away to make room for his opponents, had died away, there ensued a sudden silence on the hustings. The county magnates looked from one to another inquiringly, but no response was attempted. The tall Sir Hillsborough Tomkins, one of the leaders of the opposition, was gossiping in an unconcerned manner with the stout Colonel Tilbury, an equally influential chief of the same party, and the ever active little Dr. Potts of the Royal Navy, was quietly listening to the last newly invented old joke of Captain Doldrum, the heaviest of heavy dragoons in the British Army. They were among the *elite* of "the Pinks," and were believed to belong to the committee to whom had been entrusted the management of the unknown candidate's election. But neither advanced to the front of the hustings.

The High Sheriff now came forward, and demanded to know if any elector intended to propose any other candidate. The mob below pressed forward, looking intensely curious, and the "True Blues" above whispered together, apparently a little anxious; but their opponents made no sign. The High Sheriff then, amid profound silence, declared John Drelincourt, Esq., of "the Hall" duly elected member for Blankshire, in the room of the Honourable Albert Frederick Philip Leigh, commonly called Viscount Cassington.

Everybody seemed taken by surprise by this termination of the proceedings, but no one seemed dissatisfied except certain of the county magnates, who had shrunk from putting forward their pretensions on the "True Blue" interest from a conviction that there would be a most expensive contest.

It was evident that probable candidates of the other party had been kept back by similar fears—the lavish display, and the increasing popularity of "the new man" having alarmed them, and when the committee ascertained that he had purchased, on the eve of the nomination, their particular organ, "the Blankshire Guardian," the ground seemed cut from under their feet, and it was at once resolved that there should be no opposition.

When the cheering had subsided that followed the announcement, the new member came before his constituents to return thanks, which he did with the same tact that had marked his previous speech. He prudently abstained from any reference to his opponents, and as wisely kept from uttering any pledges to his supporters, but mingled a large amount of general professions with a display of good humour and frankness that seemed to satisfy every one.

A marked change had taken place in the disposition of a considerable portion of the crowd. Even the privileged badgerers found their vocation too difficult to maintain. A broad-grinning chaw-bacon ventured to ask the successful candidate how he got on with the rookery, when he was directed to shut his ugly tater-trap by so many fierce neighbours that he wisely did not press the question. And a fat old quaker, having in a solemn manner desired to know what was to be done with the Church rates, immediately had his broad-brimmed beaver crushed down upon his head, over eyes, nose, and mouth, while in his frantic efforts at release, he got jostled about and laughed at, till he found him self far out of hearing, receiving the awkward assistance and pathetic condolences of officious friends, from whom he was only too glad to escape.

After the usual ceremonies had been concluded, there was a break-up, both of the throng on the hustings, and the mob below it. The more active friends of the new member for the county, eagerly improvised a procession through the principal thoroughfares of Pudborough,—not only to the special delight of the Pudboroughites who thronged the windows and doors of the High Street, the London Street, Victoria Square, the Cathedral Close especially,—but to the infinite gratification of the Blankshire voters and non-voters, who had on that day so largely swelled the population of the town.

All the bands were brought into requisition, and as they were not very far apart from each other, the general effect was considered to be "stunning," without much exaggeration. All the vehicles were pressed into service, but the one which divided public attention with the open landau in which the new member stood bowing to the fair of Pudborough, as they waved their choicest lace or cambric enthusiastically towards him, was the four-horse drag of Sir Charles Forrester, who preceded it, the steeple-chasers exerting themselves immensely on the roof in cheering and waving hats, while Lord Adolphus Fitzpatrick on the box was extending his cheeks most cherubically, in frantic efforts to make everybody appreciate his performance of "See the Conquering Hero comes."

The difficulties against which his lordship was contending may be faintly imagined when it is remembered that the entire male assemblage, juvenile and adult, were engaged in outshouting each other—that just before him the Pudborough brass band were deafening all around them with "There's a Good Time Coming;" that the Blankshire tea-totallers just behind him were deafening every one with "Cheer Boys, Cheer;" that a military band from the barracks under the mayor's windows, which the procession was passing, made the place resound with "The Girl I left behind Me;" while that of the Blankshire Volunteers, engaged by Mr. Drelincourt's Committee, stood before the Rose and Crown opposite, doing "God Save the Queen," with at least equal effect.

Then it must not be supposed that the music of a humbler kind, which the visitors had brought with them, remained silent. The crowded caravans swelled the harmonious Babel with their several contributions; added to which the miners broke out into a chorus, in innumerable keys, of "Rule Britannia;" and the agricultural labourers and mechanics set up a choral opposition of a similar character to the less patriotic, but equally inspiring, tune, "We won't go home till morning."

It may therefore readily be imagined that the solo of the handsome Irishman was overpowered by the terrible opposition it had to encounter, and was hardly audible even to his companions. Nevertheless, the cordial cries from them of "Go it, Fitz!" "Blow away, Old Fellow!" and many others equally encouraging, made the amateur imagine that he possessed an audience, and he persevered under these astounding difficulties with a display of wind and patience equally amazing.

Never had Pudborough known such a scene of excitement without ill-feeling being a large element in it. For once Pinks and True Blues made up an electioneering crowd, without showing the slightest disposition to come to blows; indeed, the taverns and beershops were constantly filled with political opponents fraternizing over quarts of ale, and shaking hands before tumblers of stout.

Marvellous to relate there was not a broken head at either of the doctor's surgeries, or so much as a fractured arm at the county hospital; and there was such extraordinary feasting and drinking during the day,—every respectable inhabitant apparently keeping open house for his country friends,—that the tradesmen who furnished the supplies had never before made such a harvest. In short, it was universally acknowledged that if there had ever occurred one day that deserved to be specially remembered at Pudborough, it was the day that Squire Drelincourt was returned for the county.

CHAPTER XI.

LORD VALLANCE'S LITTLE GAME.

"HEARTS are trumps! Do me the favour to remember that Hearts are trumps! Adorable creature, it is your lead. Inestimable woman, you will have to play last but one, so play your best card of the suit; if you can, play a better card than mine, or trump higher than me, if you cannot follow suit. Dummy plays last, and as I display Dummy's hand, you can ascertain at a glance what he will be obliged to play."

This little speech came from Lord Vallance—a very much improved Lord Vallance, with as extensive restorations as ever satisfied a picture dealer or a Cathedral Chapter. He sat, whiskers and wig complete, in his dressing gown and slippers, with his glass at his eye, looking quite as well as could be expected after the severe attack from which his lordship had so long suffered; sitting quite at home in one of the kitchen arm-chairs, evidently feeling quite at home, playing a game at whist on the kitchen table of the Grange.

Strange as it might appear to behold that celebrated personage playing cards in such a place at such an hour, for it was hardly noon, more extraordinary was it to notice with whom he had associated himself in the game. On his right sat Miss Charity, diligently sorting her cards, but looking the essence of middle-aged feminine contentment at finding herself so pleasantly occupied—moreover with a gentleman of such very distinguished appearance. Opposite her sat her partner, Miss Dorcas, with a tranquil sense of surprise and good-nature, looking over her spectacles at Lord Vallance as she endeavoured to understand the directions he had been giving her.

It is very easy to account for this singular juxtaposition and this novel occupation to at least two of the parties concerned. The invalid, as he grew convalescent, became more and more weary of his residence. He had his own reasons for prolonging his stay in his present quarters, uncomfortable as he must have found them, for from some cause that did not appear to his capacity of vision, no one came near him. Miss Lætitia having effected all the good in her power, had ceased to cross the threshold; the reverend gentleman, her brother, having been obliged to come to the conclusion that no spiritual benefit was practical in his case, had also ceased his visits. Professional occupation had taken away Ferdinand Stoughton, and the proprietor of the Hall found his time so completely absorbed by his own affairs, that his suffering neighbour had quite slipped out of his mind.

The poor man, therefore, found his time hang very heavily on his hands. He couldn't look out all day from the front window upon the geraniums, or from the back window on to the gooseberry bushes, and he must have something to do. He had grown exceedingly amicable with the two old domestics, since he used to shower abuse and bootjack at their inoffensive heads; and one very dull day the felicitous idea struck him that with their assistance, he would enjoy the luxury of a game at whist.

The felicitous idea was proposed to the senior, who, as she had received special instructions from her mistress to render his lordship as comfortable as possible, and from Dr. Dallas not to thwart him, if it could be avoided, only objected on the plea of her and her sister's ignorance of the game. As neither objected to being taught, the cards were produced, his lordship took Dummy against the two sisters, and the much-desired recreation became an accomplished fact.

Lord Vallance methodically sorted his partner's hand and spread it out on the table, then rapidly arranged his own cards, looking all the time with the greatest satisfaction—in short, enjoying himself immensely. His excuse was evident, he had smoked out his cigars,—he had no resource in the way of occupation or of amusement. "What was a fellow to do?"

"Dummy hasn't a bad hand, ladies. In fact, a fellow couldn't wish to have a better hand than Dummy's got. So, you see, you must finesse a little if you entertain any hope of winning."

Charity looked at the wiser sister as if to gain some knowledge from her, of what finessing meant; but Dorcas looked back over her spectacles, evidently quite as much at a loss for the meaning as herself. With the natural indecision of a beginner, the former was about to play a spade, then exchanged it for a diamond, then considered with her head on one side—then hurriedly threw down the only trump she possessed—of course playing the very last card she ought to have thought of; and Dorcas, not waiting for the next player, played the deuce of the same suit, looking as if delighted at having got rid of a card so unimportant.

Of course the teacher made her take it up again and play in her turn, and having thrown out a small trump, allowed his partner to take the trick at a very easy sacrifice. Having got the lead, the accomplished whist-player maintained it, winning trick after trick either to Dummy or himself, in a manner that quite astonished his fair antagonists. Despite of the instructions they received, they played very badly. Whether this arose from confusion of mind or inability to understand what was meant, is immaterial. Lord Vallance seemed in a fair way of getting all the tricks.

"Now, most seraphic of women, you must play a heart!" said his lordship, addressing Sister Dorcas, who, looking over her spectacles at him, triumphantly produced the king. Dummy's ace came down upon it directly.

"Have you a heart, superlative creature?" inquired Lord Vallance.

Sister Charity felt flurried; she fancied that there was a hidden meaning in the question, and then his lordship looked at her so particularly through his eye-glass. But after shuffling her cards about a good deal, and dropping half of them, she was obliged to admit, very much against her will, that she had no heart.

"Play anything you like, most celestial of females!"

At once she put down the ace of diamonds, and of course, saw it added to the heap that had been so rapidly progressing.

As Dummy's hand was now all trumps, and Sister Dorcas had only one or two small ones, the remainder of the tricks of course increased the pile, and that game was concluded, Lord Vallance announcing it as a double.

Having shuffled the pack and cut, he passed the cards to the next dealer.

Sister Charity had dealt cards before easily enough, but then there was no Lord Vallance close to her looking at her through his eye-glass, and making the most extravagant professions of admiration, as he directed her where to put the cards. Notwithstanding all such attentions, at the end she discovered that she had misdealt, and with as much philosophy as she could assume, permitted his lordship to gather up the several hands, shuffle them together, cut himself, and deal them out.

"Over seven or under seven!" exclaimed the accomplished player, before he had turned the last card. "Unparalleled feminine paragon, what will you bet?" he added, turning to the elder, who merely laughed as she glanced over her spectacles.

He then turned to the other.

"Sublimest of sublunary angels, lay me a wager that the card is over seven? or if you like, is under that number?"

"What ought I to lay, my Lord?" cried the spinster, simpering, and quite unable to resist so touching an appeal.

"O! sometimes people will bet a hundred pounds!"

"That is quite impossible, my Lord," cried Sister Dorcas, gravely.

"Haven't got so much tin, eh? Well, say a pony."

"Sister Charity never had a pony of her own in her life, my Lord," said the elder, again with much seriousness of manner.

"I used to ride Uncle Dick's 'grey' when I was very young," put in the younger, with a small assumption of dignity.

Lord Vallance first turned his eye-glass on one and then on the other, with an intense expression of astonishment.

"Is it possible such miraculous verdure can exist anywhere?" he at last cried.

"If your Lordship pleases," said Dorcas,

as if anxious to gratify a gentleman who had condescended to sit down to play a game at cards with her and her sister. "If your Lordship would permit, my sister and myself would bet sixpence each!"

"That's dreadfully low. I don't think that would suit my book. But playing a little game may be better for a fellow than doing nothing. It's quite ridiculous, my inapproachable cherubims; but now, do you mean to bet on the card being over seven or under seven?"

"If you please my Lord, my sister will take it one way, and I the other!"

Lord Vallance gazed at the woman apparently astounded.

"You don't say so! That would be uncommon profitable to me, for I should stand safe to win nothing and to lose nothing. The sixpences must trot together, rarest of hen phœnixes."

"I'm sure I don't care which wager I take," here observed Charity, "but I should prefer doing the same as Dorcas."

The more prudent senior made no further objection, and it was agreed that they should both bet sixpence that the card was under seven. The wager was at once accepted by the dealer, the card was turned up, and proved to be a seven of spades.

Lord Vallance looked at the card at first as if dubious, then gazed as fixedly on the two old dames, who seemed respectfully waiting his decision; finally he appeared quite decided.

"Most angeliferous of women, you have both lost," he presently exclaimed.

The sisters evidently did not comprehend this.

"A fellow can see it with half an eye. Nothing can be clearer. Just look here, you splendacious creature."

Lord Vallance turned to one.

"You bet, Lord Vallance, the card is over seven. The card is turned up, and it is not over seven; therefore you lose!"

He now turned to the other.

"Then you, divinest of seraphs, lay Lord Vallance the same wager, and consequently lose it in identically the same way."

"Oh! very well my Lord, I shall be quite happy to pay your Lordship whenever your

Lordship will be good enough to accept the sum."

"All right, model of feminine excellence!" he cried, proceeding to sort his cards, and those of his imaginary partner, with a running commentary of instruction to his still well-pleased opponents that seemed fresh from the last edition of Hoyle.

It was now Dorcas's lead, and whether it was that she, the more sensible of the sisters, began to see her way into the game, or that she held a better hand than before, she began by winning three tricks in succession, which caused her to glance at her right-honourable adversary over her spectacles, with an expression of mingled good-humour and triumph. She played ace, king, and queen of the same suit. Sister Charity seemed to reflect the satisfaction of Sister Dorcas, and looked as if she too could be equally successful when her opportunity arrived.

The accomplished card-player turned his eye-glass from one to the other, then scanned his partner's hand, and then his own, then caressed his whiskers and looked up to the ceiling like one making a calculation. The leader, as she had done so well, thought she might continue her success, and still more triumphantly played the knave of the same suit.

"Sister Dorcas, if clubs had been trumps, you would have had all the honours!" exclaimed Sister Charity, with admiring astonishment.

"So she would, superlative woman!" answered Lord Vallance. "But as diamonds were turned up, honours won't count in that suit. Dummy plays the four. If you've got a club you must play it, or revoke."

Charity looked in alarm at her sister, who, too, did not seem quite easy in her mind—neither having the slightest idea what was meant, but being apprehensive that it meant mischief. Under this feeling the younger seemed undecided, then desperately trumped her partner's trick with the deuce of diamonds. Lord Vallance played a higher trump, and took the trick!

Charity looked at Dorcas, and Dorcas at Charity, as if not quite satisfied with the transaction.

"Always play your best when third player, astonishingly sublime female!" observed the accomplished card-player. "And when obliged to take your partner's trick, do all your little possible to make it safe."

"Now, ladies!" he added, "I will draw it singularly mild for you. I play the deuce of hearts."

Again Dorcas glanced triumphant as she threw down the king. Dummy's ace followed, of course, and then fell the queen.

Now his lordship played the knave of the same suit, Dorcas followed suit, but as Dummy could not, the other players expected that it would be trumped, but a small card of a different suit was played, and the ten falling from the remaining hand the trick followed the last.

Lord Vallance, however, did not have it entirely his own way during the remainder of the game. His opponents held very good cards, and though he frequently glanced speculatively at the ceiling, and the old women played badly, he could not help the trick being won occasionally by the best card. Still the game took a longer time than the last; and the sisters were within one point of winning it, but from that point they were never suffered to advance, and at last they lost the game.

"Single, double, and the rub!" exclaimed Lord Vallance, drawing the cards together.

Again Charity looked at Dorcas, and Dorcas at Charity, but without either gaining anything by the transaction.

"If you please, my Lord," asked the other, timidly, "what may that mean?"

"It means that each of you owe me five guineas."

Both jumped from their seats with the most lively consternation expressed in their round faces.

"Five guineas, my Lord!" they cried in a breath.

"Every fellow plays guinea points," observed his lordship, calmly. "And there's the first game, which was double; the second, which was single; and the game, which counts two more, you know. And Dummy, being my partner, of course I take for Dummy. That's ten guineas in all, according to Cocker."

"Ten guineas!" repeated Dorcas, looking in a slight degree alarmed.

"Ten guineas!" echoed Charity, as though quite bewildered.

"That's the sum, exactly, divinest of your sex! But what's that noise?"

A knocking at the outer door was heard, which the two attendants from their painful pre-occupation not immediately noticing, it was presently repeated more loudly; and then, without waiting for the door being opened, a middle-aged man, with a keen sharp look, wearing a dusty suit of black, entered, with an umbrella in one hand and a hat in the other. He cast a searching glance rapidly round the room, and then fixed his gaze on Lord Vallance, who had risen from his chair, and was examining the stranger through his eye-glass from head to foot.

"Your servant, my Lord!" he exclaimed, with a sweep of his arm intended to do duty as a bow. "I hope that I have the honour of seeing your Lordship well."

"You have the advantage of me," replied Lord Vallance, calmly, but eyeing the intruder evidently with a strong feeling of distrust.

"Just so, exactly," replied the man, with a particularly cheerful air. "The members of our profession do sometimes have a slight advantage when brought in contact with such distinguished individuals as your Lordship."

"Have the goodness to tell me your business."

"Quite a simple matter, my Lord, I assure you—the most simple matter in the world. I am directed by a lady——"

"You come from Lady Vallance?"

"I have the honour of being her ladyship's legal adviser."

"Precisely."

"Moreover, my client is waiting at the door, with the hope of renewing her conjugal relations with your Lordship. Have I your Lordship's permission to bring you together? It would give me infinite pleasure."

"Of course, my good sir, nothing would be more agreeable to me. I shall be infinitely obliged to you."

The gentleman in black, with the cordial smile of a philanthropist on an errand of humanity, put his umbrella under his arm, hastened to the door, and quickly returned, bringing in a fashionably dressed lady, closely veiled, wearing a very wide skirt, and a pink bonnet, a blue mantle, and carrying a mauve parasol. She made a spring as she entered, but when she caught sight of Lord Vallance, evidently hesitated, stood still, then advanced slowly a little nearer, and stood still again, swinging her parasol.

Lord Vallance appeared to be watching her progress towards himself through his eye-glass, with much the same curiosity that he would have regarded the movements of a wild beast in a cage. The two old women looked on, too bewildered to make any comment.

Lord Vallance advanced a step as the lady threw up her veil and disclosed a face that did not in the slightest degree resemble that of Lady Vallance. She stared at him with something of the expression of a tiger-cat, entertaining a doubt regarding the character of the prey on which she had been about to make a spring. Lord Vallance continued to scrutinize her features without showing the slightest sign of recognition; then he looked inquiringly at her companion, very much as if wondering what it all meant.

The sharp-visaged female seemed to be putting some powerful restraint upon her feelings. The husband she sought she knew very well had had different coloured hair, and a totally different complexion, when she had known him fifteen years before. And yet there was something in Lord Vallance which reminded her of the Honourable Sylvester Howard, but she could not tell what it was.

Her companion had expected to have seen marks of confusion in the countenance of the person he had come to visit; but his sharpest scrutiny could detect there nothing of the kind; the confusion seemed to be only in the face of his client, who seemed as it were struck dumb with surprise.

"You remember this lady, Lord Vallance?"

"Never saw her before."

"Indeed, my Lord! Then you have totally forgotten one Lucretia Jefferson Stickles whom your Lordship married in the year—— at a place called Sticklesville, in the United States of America."

"Never heard of such a person, and never was in America in my life."

Mr. Prodd seemed taken aback a little;

his client a good deal more so; Dorcas and Charity continued silent and amazed.

"Then you absolutely mean to tell me, Lord Vallance," exclaimed the lawyer, reluctant to regard the case as one of mistaken identity, "that you never went by the name of the Honourable Sylvester Howard?"

Lord Vallance broke out into a genuine laugh.

Mr. Prodd looked rather savage, and Miss Lucretia black and vindictive.

"I see it now plain enough. Sylvester's my younger brother, and always was a deuce of a fellow for getting into scrapes. I remember quite well that he once made a tour in the United States; but whether he got spliced there I am not in a position to say, as he never told me, and I couldn't know it, you know, without. But he wasn't considered a bit like me in anything. I'm therefore monstrously surprised that I should be taken for him."

Mr. Prodd mused, but seemed disinclined to acknowledge himself mistaken.

"Surely, madam, you must have sufficient

recollection of your husband to be able to say whether this gentleman is or is not the man."

"I'm in a fix about it, that's a fact," replied the governess, somewhat sulkily.

"If you are not convinced by my simple denial," observed Lord Vallance, with the most frank manner possible, "there is Mr. Drelincourt, a magistrate, lives close by. If you wait while I change my coat and put on my boots, I will go with you to him. But really the thing is monstrous ridiculous, you know, for I'm no more like my brother than I'm like the Pope."

The proposition to go before a magistrate both lawyer and client considered the last thing a man charged with a felony would have proposed. Mr. Prodd felt that there was no evidence in his possession which would sanction his giving such a person in charge on such an offence; but if Lord Val lance went before a magistrate voluntarily, he should have no responsibility in the matter, and might bring forward what he knew of the case, or not, just as he pleased.

So Mr. Prodd accepted the proposal, and

Lord Vallance laughingly saying his toilet would not detain them long, went out of the room, and was heard going up the stair-case, humming an opera air. The lawyer cautiously strode after him, and threw open the door, so that his lordship could not descend without being seen.

"It's very strange, madam, that you cannot identify him. Very awkward, too. Lady Vallance has been detained by an accident on the line, but even were she here, I don't see how a charge of bigamy could be sustained, unless you can swear positively that Lady Vallance's husband was previously married to you. If you married the younger brother, it's impossible that you could have married Lord Vallance."

"It doesn't convene for me to swear I married Lord Vallance," replied the lady with considerable irritation. "All that I can swear is, that I was married to the Honourable Sylvester Howard."

"That's not exactly the evidence my client requires, madam," replied the gentleman in the dusty clothes, somewhat testily.

"I guess your client ain't of much account to me," retorted his companion.

"You're equally interested in the case?"

"No we ain't. I didn't marry any woman's husband, I reckon."

"It is not necessary for the ends of justice, that you should have done so. All that is wanted is, that you should both have been induced to marry the same man in the life-time of the other."

"Nor do I want to take away any woman's husband," she added, with an indignant toss of her pink bonnet.

"My client has no intention of the kind, madam. Her object is to get rid of him. If you can prove your prior right, you may take him and welcome, when the law has done with him; but your inability to identify a person with whom you say you have lived on the most affectionate of domestic relations till he mysteriously disappeared before the end of the honey-moon, is really, madam, most extraordinary."

"I tell you man, he's fixed up quite different!" cried the governess, angrily.

The lawyer continued to complain of her deficiency as a witness, and she continued to display her irritation at his remarks,—Dorcas and Charity still looking on and listening, without taking the slightest share in the dispute.

" Is not Lord Vallance a long time getting ready ?" suddenly inquired Mr. Prodd, when some twenty minutes at least had been expended in the altercation.

Dorcas asked if she should go and knock at his door, and receiving permission, at once departed on her errand. Charity remained, apparently too interested in the strange scene going on, to desire to leave it for a moment. Mr. Prodd renewed his complaints, and Miss Stickles her retorts, both evidently getting more and more irritable.

In this way more than five minutes elapsed unperceived by either of the contending parties, before Dorcas returned.

" If you please, sir," she said, with a mild glance of astonishment over her spectacles, " Lord Vallance isn't up stairs at all, sir."

The words acted on both with equal violence.

"Bolted!" cried Mr. Prodd, and firmly replacing his dusty hat on his head, and grasping the oil-skin of his umbrella, he rushed out at the open door, and sprung up-stairs.

"Skedaddled!" exclaimed Miss Stickles simultaneously, as she held her voluminous skirts with one hand, seized her parasol by the other, and rushed after the lawyer. Both evidently entertained the same conviction.

There ensued such a rushing to and fro up-stairs—such a banging of doors, such a rummaging of drawers and cupboards, such knocking about of furniture, as made the two ancient attendants fearful that everything up-stairs was being broken to pieces.

Presently down came Mr. Prodd flying over the stairs, and running through the kitchen like a madman. In another moment, the equally frantic Miss Stickles sped after him, at a similar reckless pace. Lord Vallance's flight satisfied both that they were on the right track, and marvellous were their exertions to follow up the pursuit.

Dorcas and Charity beheld the strange chase with equal amazement. They hurried to the door to see where their visitors were going, and were just in time to catch a glimpse of a balloon-like figure disappearing at an angle of the road. It was the last either ever saw of Miss Lucretia Jefferson Stickles, or of Mr. Prodd, Attorney-at-Law.

They had also seen the last of the accomplished card-player, who had so condescended to teach them how to play at whist. How he got out of the house, how he contrived to disappear without leaving the slightest trace of his departure, remained a mystery; till some time after the return of the tenant of the Grange certain articles of her mother's wardrobe were missed, and it became known that Sir Charles Forrester, while driving his team along the high-road at a little distance from the Grange, had been hailed by an old lady with a travelling-bag, and accepting the idea as a capital joke, had allowed her to take a seat inside the drag, and had driven her to the next railway station.

Lord Vallance had, there was no reason to doubt, hastily disguised himself in the deceased lady's clothes, and having dropped unperceived from the back-window, easily reached the high-road. His lordship was never seen in that neighbourhood again.

CHAPTER XII.

CONSCIENCE CLEAR.

SUCH was the state of affairs with regard to some of our *dramatis personæ*, when Lord Lionel Leigh returned to the Hall with vague misgivings as to what might have occurred during his absence.

These were principally caused by a remembrance of his last interview with his betrothed, and the fact of her unfrequent and frigid correspondence. It was not, then, to be wondered at, if an incident which occurred near the end of his journey, affected him more strongly than it might otherwise have done.

He came suddenly upon Miss Drelincourt and

Ferdinand Stoughton riding together slowly, apparently in more interesting and confidential discourse than an engaged man cares to see between his intended bride and a male cousin. Her seat on horseback had something in it listless and dejected, different from its usual graceful carriage, whilst listening to her kinsman, as he bent beside her almost touching her pommel; but the colour which first flushed and then left her cheeks paler than Lord Lionel had ever seen them, the start which even the usually self-possessed Stoughton gave, as the long absent lover's carriage turned the corner of a road suddenly upon them, seemed to him tokens of ominous significance.

They rode by his side as far as it was possible, the conversation naturally constrained on all sides, and while the heiress's manner was either agitated or distant.

Lord Lionel was the first to reach the house, and stood on the steps awaiting their arrival, stepping forward to lift Miss Drelincourt from the saddle, with a firm yet gentle right of appropriation, under which her slight frame perceptibly trembled. She lingered for a short space after in his company with her father, then went up to her room, and did not reappear till dinner-time, when she was again apparently under some constraint, avoiding as much as possible direct communication with her lover. What she did say was more particularly addressed to her cousin who managed constantly to call her attention to himself. In his manner there was more of nervous anxiety, and less of easy assurance, than was common to him.

Mr. Drelincourt looked grave and anxious towards his daughter, as if seeing her now with her betrothed, his eyes were opened to the change in their mutual relationship; while on his nephew his glance dwelt with suspicion.

He had got over the discussion of Lady Vallance's affairs before dinner, the candid openness with which his intended son-in-law treated the subject, disabusing his generous mind of whatever distrust he might recently have entertained.

Lord Lionel passed from that subject to the question of his own marriage, to arrange which he said was the purpose of his present visit to the Hall.

"She has been looking pale of late," his intended father-in-law observed; "out of sorts, as was but natural, you know. Indeed, it was rather a tax upon a girl's faith and patience, to have her intended taking up the cudgels of another woman—a former love, too. Poor child! she had borne it as well as could be expected. Ferdinand had helped to get her through the time. Ferdinand was a kind-hearted fellow; he had been quite a brother to her."

Lord Lionel would not condescend to cast a shade of suspicion on the manner in which the young barrister might have played the part of fraternal consoler. He maintained the show of confidence, and trusted in a *téte-à-téte* with his betrothed, for having everything arranged satisfactorily.

As is often the case when men are inwardly most on the defence against one another, there was more outward mutual civility between the two gentlemen than usual, and the subject of Lord Vallance had been discussed by them over their wine after dinner very amicably.

The direct mention of Lady Vallance's name

had been as if by common consent avoided during the meal, but when Lord Lionel, who had made several attempts—which the barrister rendered abortive by engaging him on some fresh topic of conversation—to follow Miss Drelincourt, seated himself at last at her side in the drawing-room, he lowered his voice to the confidential lover's tone it had been their privilege to maintain in company,

"You have asked me no question yet," he said, "concerning your unfortunate friend Lady Vallance; has your kindly interest in her quite evaporated?"

"Friend!" she repeated, whilst she flushed and averted her face. "I scarcely know," and her voice trembled, "if that is the name I am justified in giving her. Of course, however, I am glad to hear of her probable rescue from her unfortunate predicament."

"Her situation is really a most unhappy one," Lord Lionel added gravely, still striving to see nothing in Miss Drelincourt's reserve but what a full explanation on his part would for ever obliterate.

The heiress gave him no encouragement to

pursue the theme; on the contrary, it seemed as if some influence, independently of her own feelings, made her more and more reserved in her manner. He bore it patiently till he observed a peculiar nervous glance directed at her cousin, and became aware that, though apparently occupied with his uncle, that young gentleman was evidently listening and watching them. Lord Lionel could stand it no longer, and with a flash of angry impatience from his eyes, he rose abruptly and left her.

When he looked at her again, though apparently relieved by his withdrawal, she was very pale, and the expression of her countenance unusually dejected. He did not, however, approach or address her again during the evening, though with no slight anxiety he awaited the morrow's *eclaircissement*.

The greatness of this anxiety might have surprised him some months before, when he would as soon have expected the moon to vary her phases as the calm happy nature of his betrothed to show signs of what he considered a capricious disposition. He felt much annoyed, and that not merely from a natural inclination to be piqued by a show of coldness, by a tinge of jealousy, or wounded vanity, caused by the conviction that another had usurped his place in the affections of his mistress, but because, in this altered aspect of affairs, he felt humiliated in not having been able to inspire a more durable attachment.

The next morning, after breakfast, Lord Lionel, as soon as he could make his escape from his host, who had carried him off with him to the stables, returned to the house to look for Henrietta, whom he found in her boudoir, and he then gladly availed himself of the opportunity of having the confidential communication with her that should set everything to rights which had appeared wrong.

"That cousin of yours is becoming intolerable," he said. "It is a pity he has not some employment in his profession."

Henrietta coloured.

"He has been almost my sole companion lately," she replied, looking down and hesitating. "I do not know what I should have done without him. Every one has been so absorbed—even Papa—since——"

"Well, well," Lord Lionel said, laughingly, almost glad to find the Squire included in the accusation levelled against himself, "I hope all occasion for his cousinly *devoirs* is now at an end; I want you to fix the day, dearest for our marriage. Your father and I would like it to be the first week in June. All will then be in readiness; for do not suppose I have been entirely absorbed in the concerns of others whilst away. It is useless, I know, to think of an earlier period, with the prejudice existing against the poor fated month of May."

Henrietta's face drooped silently for a moment, and the hand he had so tenderly taken, perceptibly trembled; then withdrawing it, she said in an agitated tone, "I think I should like to speak to my father first; if you will allow me, I will go to him and return presently."

Her lover looked surprised and hurt.

"Oh! certainly," he replied somewhat hastily, but I should have imagined it was a point which might have been settled with more propriety between ourselves at once, considering that the arrangement has long been tacitly made, and that your father has already spoken with me on the subject."

"It is not that exactly," she said, hesitatingly. "But indeed I would rather see him first," she added.

He turned away, and she left the room as if escaping from an embarrassing position.

Lord Lionel remained with a darkened countenance. His pride was receiving chastisement which he felt he did not deserve. Was he to be trifled with a second time?

He opened books absently that lay upon the table; then, after pacing the room restlessly for some twenty minutes, the impulse moved him to follow Miss Drelincourt to the library, and in the presence of her father to insist on the decision which she had avoided in private.

CHAPTER XIII.

A RE-UNION.

Mr. Drelincourt had been surprised by his daughter entering the library, when he had imagined the lovers shut up at least for one hour's colloquy; he was distressed to see her with such an anxious countenance, but greatly was he astounded when sinking into a chair before him, she began to sob hysterically.

"Papa, I want you to speak to Lionel," she said, in reply to his soothing words. "I really have not courage to tell him myself, but I think after all that has occurred, it would be better if matters proceeded no further between us; in fact, that our engagement should be broken off."

"What is the matter now!" cried the old gentleman. "Who the deuce has been putting all this nonsense into your head, I should like to know? "What has occurred? Why, if you mean this—this affair of my Lady Vallance, if you think, because you have discovered that you are not the first young lady Leigh has fancied, and that you have a right to feel yourself injured in consequence, by Jove, I am sorry for you! Rather be thankful that you are the only woman whom he has found capable of satisfying his ideas as to what a wife should be. Depend upon it, my dear, the knowledge that you have been selected under such circumstances, is a surer foundation for conjugal happiness than a first passion by whomsoever inspired."

"Ah! but papa, you do not know all perhaps. He loved her long and fervently; he would have married her. It was only pique at her conduct with Lord Vallance which drove him back to England to propose to me. He loves her still in his heart most probably, and having been occupied with her cause so earnestly; been with her every day, exposed to her remarkable fascinations, it is only a mere sense of honour that makes him still wish to fulfil his engagement with me."

"Fiddle-de-dee!" her father exclaimed, impatiently; "you have arrived at a very improper conclusion. What business have you to imagine anything of the sort? Because my Lord generously comes forward to befriend this foolish woman, who has got herself into a scrape, you must needs suspect him capable of treacherously carrying on an intrigue when engaged to yourself."

"But papa," the heiress insisted, wiping away her tears, "if he is always to be haunted by remembrances of the past, and if when Lord Vallance dies I am to feel that I was the obstacle to their re-union, I should not like it at all. I do not pretend to the attractions of Lady Vallance, but I do feel," she added, with a little pettish pride, "that I have the right to aspire to the supreme place in some one person's affections. Lord Lionel is too honourable I know to wish to draw back from our engagement. In a manner he may even love me, but——"

"But what, now?" Mr. Drelincourt demanded, sharply, looking keenly at his daughter's downcast countenance. "Even if it were as you say, depend upon it you would be wise to be satisfied with his affection. Sir Roger de Coverley never had a daughter to manage—his widow was womankind sufficient for him—I don't therefore wonder at his leading a life that must be the envy of generations of country gentlemen. But I don't at all like this behaviour of yours. I hope Ferdinand has not been putting these ideas into your head?"

She answered that her cousin had always been very kind to her, especially lately, when she had been unhappy; but she did not think he had put any ideas into her head.

"*I* do though," replied the old gentleman. "I see now what that fine gentleman has been about. He has been taking advantage of his late opportunity to inveigle himself into your good graces by his insinuations and innuendoes, at the expense of your lover. Are you really so very weak as to be biassed by him? If there no longer existed the affection you acknowledged for your intended husband, Lord Lionel, he would be well quit of you, but I beg leave just to say that Mr.

Ferdinand Stoughton, barrister-at-law, of the Inner Temple, shall be no longer a bar to so desirable a union. Why, don't you know it is that clever young gentleman's interest that you shall marry no one but himself. I have been fool enough to put him in the entail, in case 'you should die without children.'"

The heiress, unaccustomed to being scolded, made no remark, and looked a little out of humour.

It was at this juncture that Lord Lionel entered.

It must have gone far to chase away any misgiving that clouded the vision of one who truly loved him, when she saw him enter the apartment, with his open, truthful countenance, and the good impression ought to have been strengthened when, with firm, clear tones as he sat by her side, he apologized for his intrusion. The fact was, he owned that he was too impatient to know his fate, to bear the suspense of her absence any longer.

"And I am glad you are come," exclaimed Mr. Drelincourt, angrily, "my daughter has been bewitched, I think, while you have been away."

"Or rather 'some one'" he was too prudent to name his nephew, "has been putting into her head nonsense about this first attachment of yours."

"That nonsense may be soon done away with, I trust, if the mischief has gone no farther," answered Lord Lionel. "I had intended to make a full explanation to Henrietta just now, if she had allowed me."

The conference might have concluded satisfactorily to all parties had not the door abruptly opened, and Ferdinand made his appearance, with the announcement that Lord Vallance had suddenly disappeared, and that there was a charge against him of bigamy.

Lord Lionel listened silently, but not without signs of astonishment.

The full particulars were soon detailed, and a lively conversation followed.

Miss Drelincourt presently said in a low voice—

"Of course we shall be happy for Lady Vallance to come here if it should be any accommodation to her."

And then rising, without looking either at Lord Lionel or her cousin, she left the room.

It was quite night when a lady visitor arrived at the Hall, on foot, who, much to the surprise of the domestics, was recognized as a frequent guest there a few months before. She begged them to apprise Miss Drelincourt privately of her arrival, or to show her directly to her chamber if the young lady had retired for the night. She had therefore been taken upstairs, for Miss Drelincourt was indisposed and had remained in her own apartments all that evening.

Unannounced the once favoured guest entered the familiar *boudoir*, as its mistress sat dejected, nursing her grievance in mournful perplexity of spirit.

"Lady Vallance!" she exclaimed, in intense surprise, quite exhausted. Her visitor sunk on a low ottoman, while her former friend seemed too embarrassed to speak.

Presently, however, recovering her presence of mind she played the hostess with her usual courtesy, and her guest at once entered upon her story, and did not cease till she had fully explained her position.

The heiress heard her out patiently, and attempted a reply, but her words were constrained and formal. In spite of the fulness of the explanation she did not appear quite satisfied.

Perhaps her friend suspected the cause of this, for she looked earnestly into her pale face, and laid her hand gently upon her arm.

"And you, you are not happy?" she said, with a return to her old affectionate manner.

"I am not!" was the reply.

"Then you ought to be!" she added,—"if any one on earth deserves and has the power to be happy."

Miss Drelincourt averted her face.

"You are surely not capricious and trifling with your happiness?" inquired her friend. "If so, let me entreat you to take warning from my example and my fate."

Before the other could reply, there was a low knock at the door, and Ferdinand Stoughton entered.

He looked extremely surprised to see the dark figure by his cousin's side, whom he readily recognized; but, recovering his self-possession immediately, indeed feeling rejoiced at her reappearance on the scene for reasons of his own, he advanced and offered his hand. His courtesy, however, was not accepted. Its object only fixed her brilliant eyes on his, an instinct making her feel more strongly than ever at that moment that the man before her could never be her friend, and was likely to be her enemy.

He apologized for his intrusion, stating that he had not been made aware of Lady Vallance's arrival when he came to inquire after his cousin's health and wish her "good-night."

Then he asked if he might be permitted to inform Lord Lionel Leigh of her being in the house?

The young lady replied, coldly, that her business was with Miss Drelincourt and her father, not with Lord Lionel Leigh.

Ferdinand glancing at his cousin, bowed and withdrew. There was something in the lady's look and manner that made him feel ill at ease. He did not understand what it meant. There was just a possibility that it might mean him no good.

"Something assures me, my dear Miss Drelincourt," observed her guest, "that the gentleman who has just favoured me with his absence has something to do with the unsatisfactory state of your affairs. He was never a favourite of mine—indeed, I never could help experiencing a certain feeling of distrust when in his company. Did I not warn you—I intended to have done so—against him? Do not look offended at my speaking thus of your cousin, but answer truly, are not my words fully justified? Has he not been striving to undermine your faith in Lord Lionel by insinuations and representations, or rather misrepresentations, respecting myself and Lord Lionel; in short, making a clear stage for his own advancement?"

Miss Drelincourt's head drooped lower and lower, her cheeks mantling with a deeper glow. She could not deny that such had been the case.

"Lady Vallance!" she said, falteringly.

"Do not call me by that hateful name. Thank God I have no right to it."

The heiress flung herself into her friend's arms, pride and suspicion giving way before her returning affection—and she wept freely.

"My dear Miss Mauleverer," she tenderly murmured, taking her friend's hand between her own, "do not think it is entirely my cousin or my own selfish feeling which has influenced me in this matter. If I have deemed it best to give up Lionel, it is because I foresee a future now opening for him—for you, with which I have not courage to interfere. You have lost nothing. He who once loved you, must love you again when the obstacles are removed which separate you; and whoever once loved Lionel must love him to eternity."

The unimpassioned look which had been fixed upon Miss Drelincourt vanished as these words were faltered out.

"Forgive me," she said; "if you can speak thus, I have misjudged you, and all will be right. Hear my last words on the subject—Love such as that with which Lionel and I have loved *cannot* be renewed in this life. I leave to you the rest. Now, allow me once more to embrace you, and let me go to my room."

She saw no one else that night.

Lord Lionel received in silence Stoughton's announcement of the new arrival. The Squire concluded that his visitor would prefer being left to his daughter for that evening, and only sent up a message expressive of kindly satisfaction that she had availed herself once more of his hospitality. Ferdinand made another effort to see his cousin again, but in vain. His little game looked desperate.

CHAPTER XIV.

THE LAST WALK.

As on the first morning of her walk from the Hall, Julia Mauleverer dressed herself in haste in her dark-flowing garments, glided again downwards and from the house, once more in the direction of the Grange.

And again, as on that memorable morning, she was followed—again joined, escorted on her way by the same companion, Lord Lionel Leigh. It was in this instance a parting, rather than a meeting, for nothing was said by either that was not expressive of their eternal separation. His Lordship returned to the Hall in time for a somewhat early breakfast hour, but still to find Ferdinand

Stoughton on the watch, apparently looking out for a last chance.

Miss Drelincourt shortly after entered the room with her father, who seemed more hearty and genial than ever. Her colour varied beautifully from white rose to red; and her eyes were downcast, otherwise there were apparent but very slight traces of indisposition.

She had been under the hands of an excellent physician. Lord Lionel was silent and grave, and Ferdinand Stoughton not half satisfied. His cousin seemed no longer to feel his eye upon her; she scarce heard him when he spoke, apparently was too much occupied in coaxing back the warm affection of her father, and watching almost anxiously for word or look from Lord Lionel.

The clever man of the world was growing more uneasy while affecting to be unconcerned, yet was the most talkative if not the most agreeable member of the party. He felt a little anxious about what would happen after breakfast. If he could manage to get his cousin once more alone, he would try his chances.

On rising from the table, his fair kinswoman was about to retire to her own apartments, and as Lord Lionel showed no intention of following her, he was about availing himself of the opportunity, when his uncle, as if divining his motives, seized his arm and carried him off to the stables.

When an hour later he was released, he made his way to his cousin's boudoir, ostensibly to inquire whether she had any commands for the neighbouring town, whither he was going to ride, and he came upon the

"Sight hateful, sight tormenting,"

to one under his state of hope deferred; if not exactly of "those two unparadised in each other's arms," at least, in such an attitude of lover-like reconciliation and renewed confidence, as struck home to him at once the complete conviction that the game was up for him, *now* and for ever. He departed as suddenly as he came.

When later in the day, he at last found himself close to Henrietta,—Lord Lionel making no effort to prevent it,—he attempted to congratulate her on her return to her old impressions, and said something intended to be sarcastic—of her generous forgiveness of sins.

"Yes, Ferdinand," she answered, quietly, "I have acted very foolishly, and was extremely jealous. You were very kind, I am sure; I shall never forget it; but that is all over, and we will not speak of it again."

"Quite right," he replied, with what consolation he could.

A parting cousinly salute was gallantly proffered and laughingly accepted, and the next day Ferdinand Stoughton returned to his club, and bachelor's accommodations in the Temple, for the Squire hinted—and indeed without that hint, he would not most certainly have thought it worth while to remain—that as in a week's time he was going to town, it would be just as well for the lovers to be left undisturbed.

So it was arranged, and Lord Lionel and his fair *fiancée* were seen riding out together, enjoying the remnant of their courtship with the best wishes of every one who met them.

CHAPTER XV.

THE ZEALOUS CURATE OBTAINS PREFERMENT.

The Reverend Septimus Fairholme ought to have been a happy man. He stood in great favour with his Bishop—in great favour with his patron—in great favour with his parish. His zeal, his single-mindedness, his sincerity, were appreciated everywhere. The new buildings that were to be so remarkable an addition to the few architectural attractions of Middlecombe-Regis—thanks to the business habits of his munificent friend, who looked after the contract for their erection—were proceeding most satisfactorily, and the professional resources of Mr. Vitruvius Palladio Crockett were being displayed with a fair amount of satisfactory effect.

To be sure there was some rather sharp criticisms upon certain salient features of the design in the columns of the *Builder*, and the account of it appended to the engraving in the *Illustrated London News* did not contain anything that could be taken as commendation; but there had been a controversy going on about it for some time in the two county papers, that had attracted a good deal of attention in Blankshire; and a paper had been read about it at the "Ecclesiological Society," which plunged all Anglican archæologists up to their ears in mediæval antiquities.

The fact is, the eminent firm of Crockett and Finial having duly ascertained that ample funds were forthcoming, could not avoid the temptation of drawing up their plans in such a manner as would secure the architects the largest professional remuneration attainable out of such a work; consequently, they had prepared a miniature cathedral for the parish church, a pocket ecclesiastical palace for the rectory, and a diamond edition of a monastery for the schools.

The general effect was, of course, quite imposing, the details were exceedingly attractive, and, in short, it was the opinion of every one who had, or who fancied he had, either knowledge or taste, that so remarkable a structure had not been designed in the present age—an age, by the way, singularly fruitful in remarkable structures. The most antiquarian young gentlemen pronounced it "prodigiously fine for a new place," and the most æsthetic young ladies gushingly declared it to be "*so* exquisitely ancient, and *so* sweetly pretty!"

Despite such flattering opinions, the zealous Curate, during the progress of the building, not only had to undergo the troubles inseparable from bricks and mortar, but continually found himself in a less pleasant element, for he was constantly in hot water. One day an angry letter appeared in the columns of the *Blankshire Guardian,* calling the attention of all true Protestants of the Reformed Church of England to the insidious but most alarming attempt that was being made to introduce Popish practices into a quiet country village, and severely denouncing certain specified novelties that were in progress not a hundred miles from the rural parish of Middlecombe-Regis.

Mr. Fairholme had hardly completed a calm reply to this exceedingly indignant "Anglicus," when a still more indignant "Laicus" attacked him in the *Blankshire Telegraph*, for his Papistical innovations, with greater fierceness. The Reverend Septimus lost no time in defending the rood-screen, in the same temperate manner he had just defended the organ-loft and the credence-table; but the next week half a dozen dreadfully indignant correspondents appeared in each newspaper, using the most inflammatory language, while denouncing other objectionable features in the same structure.

"Anti-Jesuit" was particularly personal; "Anti-Puseyite" quite abusive; "A True Protestant" was guilty of gross exaggeration; "No-Popery" intolerably offensive; and the rest of the pack barked at the architect, the incumbent, the patron, ay, even the Bishop, like hounds in full cry.

The badgered Incumbent lost no time in taking up the cudgels in his own defence. Mr. Vitruvius Palladio Crockett wrote two columns in defence of the building and its designer, Mr. Drelincourt sent a few modest words excusing himself, and the Bishop's Chaplain published a stinging reply on behalf of his diocesan. But in the following week both papers were filled with still more indignant effusions, and leading articles appeared in the *Telegraph* and *Guardian,* admirably adapted to increase the growing irritation, and the sale of both papers.

Nothing daunted, the zealous Curate took up his pen to answer his assailants, but was interrupted in his task by a visit from Lady Theodosia Scrymgeour and the estimable prelate,—of whom her ladyship took such exceeding care,—with not only his examining chaplain, but a much more important personage in the ecclesiastical affairs of the diocese, the venerable Dean of the Cathedral of Pudborough.

The good Bishop was evidently a little alarmed at the storm that had been raised about the parish church, the venerable Dean was evidently for concessions. Lady Theodosia was for carrying things with a high hand, and the examining chaplain was for supporting

Lady Theodosia. They all carefully examined the features that had been so fiercely objected to by the terribly indignant Anglicus, Laicus, Anti-Jesuit, Anti-Puseyite, &c., &c., but apparently nothing could be less alarming than their appearance. The Bishop praised everything, and expressed a high opinion of the Incumbent, but counselled moderation. The venerable Dean was reserved. He thought a large cathedral in the county town quite enough for the county, and preferred a parish church of a simpler structure, for a quiet place like Middlecombe Regis.

Lady Theodosia opened her mind freely to Miss Lætitia, and much gratified that affectionate sister and very earnest Christian, by the uncompromising character of her opinions on officious interference with the proceedings of clergymen acting with the high sanction of their Bishop, but privately informed her that the Chapter had expressed a desire to have some alterations made in the interior of the new church, ostensibly for the purpose of allaying the popular excitement.

In a few days Mr. Fairholme received a private communication from Dr. Crumpe, mildly suggesting several alterations in the arrangement of particular portions of the sacred edifice. It was a friendly note, and the concessions, the Bishop said, did not effect the general design in the least, while they would have the advantage of removing the conscientious scruples of the "weaker brethren."

In consequence of this interposition, the parish church of Middlecombe Regis when finished, was a little less like a miniature cathedral than it might have been; nevertheless it was really a very elegant structure, and so was the rectory.

When Lady Theodosia was shown over the latter edifice, the day the Bishop consecrated the new church, by the attentive and well-satisfied Curate, she praised all its arrangements with her usual fluency of expression.

"There is only one thing wanted to make it perfect," said her ladyship, with impressive condescension. "And I am free to confess my surprise, Mr. Fairholme, that so excellent a parish priest, as I know you to be, should have sanctioned its omission."

"Dear me, Lady Theodosia!" cried the

Curate, apparently in a little alarm. "I assure your ladyship that I was unaware that anything had been forgotten. Pray tell me what ought to be added to the structure."

"*A wife*, Mr. Fairholme," replied Lady Theodosia, with particular emphasis, and looking with all the solemnity of a Bishop's lady lecturing a clerical offender. "You can never expect your influence as a minister to be properly extended in your parish, till you possess the highest domestic and moral claim on the respect of the community. Remember that, Mr. Fairholme, remember that. Now, if you please, we will join the Bishop."

The words sunk deep into the Curate's heart, and not without leaving a lasting impression. Indeed the emotions they created remained long after Dr. Crumpe had, in his most friendly episcopal way, shaken hands with him before he sprung into his carriage.

But if he was more than usually reserved during dinner, Miss Lætitia was no less so. Instead of the quiet current of parochial intelligence which usually flowed from her tongue as she ladled the soup and carved the mutton for her brother, and set him a good example by her thorough enjoyment of her meal, she ate little and talked less. Indeed it was easy to see that that really strong-minded woman was succumbing for once in her active life, to some human weakness. She had lost her spirits and her appetite.

In his pre-occupation the reverend gentleman did not notice the look of painful interest with which he was regarded, when his affectionate guardian raised her eyes from her brother's well filled plate to his thoughtful face; nor did he observe that she was doing little more in the eating way than crumbling her bread absently and occasionally putting pieces in her mouth to make a pretence of mastication, and then taking a draught of water from her tumbler, as if to dislodge the trifle from her throat.

To her the meal must have appeared unusually long. It was so different from the cheerful way it had hitherto been shared by them. Once or twice she sighed, and on one occasion there was a moisture about her eyes as if her emotions were trying to find vent in that direction; but apparently she was able to subdue such feminine infirmities, and when the final grace had been said, and the dinner things removed, she was able to take her work, and sit opposite her brother with her usual air of serenity, while he caught up the *Blankshire Telegraph* to look more closely into the "No Popery" agitation which he had contrived to excite in its columns.

"O Lætitia! has old Mrs. Barnes had the soup I directed to be sent to her?" he inquired suddenly.

"Yes, Septimus."

"And did you forward the new books of the lending library to the Miss Thompsons?"

"Yes, Septimus."

"And did the roll of flannel go to Deborah Green?"

"Yes, Septimus."

"And were you able to get any medicine for Tommy Giles?"

"Yes, Septimus."

It ought to have struck the Curate that there was something exceedingly strange in this brief and uniform answer, so different to the copiously communicative replies he had been in the habit of receiving from his zealous assistant. But his pre-occupation rendered him more unobservant than usual.

"O Lætitia!" he presently commenced again, but in a less unconcerned tone, "Lady Theodosia says I ought to marry."

"At last!" thought his sister.

"The Bishop said much the same thing to me, Septimus," she answered, and seemed to devote herself to her work with increased earnestness.

"Did his Lordship? Well, as a minister I am bound to respect the suggestions of my diocesan. But there are no directions of the kind in the Rubric—or in the Thirty-nine Articles."

His sister continued her work vigorously. but silently.

"Was his Lordship at all earnest about it?"

"Very earnest, Septimus."

"So was Lady Theodosia. I suppose it must be; but really, Lætitia, I haven't the slightest idea how it is to be brought about." The Curate having expressed this opinion, looked helplessly at his sister.

That strong-minded woman made an

audible gulp, as if something was choking her, but did not raise her eyes.

"There are plenty of young ladies in the neighbourhood," she said, "I should think it would not be difficult for you to make a selection."

"I dare say there are many estimable persons amongst them, but I have only regarded them as part of my parochial flock."

The more attentive of his fair congregation, would perhaps not have been quite satisfied with this opinion.

"Penelope Smith is very serious."

"O yes! and is regular in her attendance on all occasions, but she turns up her toes when she walks, which I do not like at all."

The three Misses Bellowes are very genteel, and their mamma is a perfect gentlewoman," added Miss Lætitia.

"Yes, they all walk gracefully; indeed I do not know any young ladies who walk so well. They are also prepossessing, especially the youngest, but they seem much too fond of showing their fine teeth. I should not like my wife to be mistaken for the walking advertisement of a cheap dentist."

"Rebecca Wood is exceedingly accomplished, Septimus."

"Yes, Lætitia, but I do not want a young person to overcome astounding difficulties on the piano without a book, to manufacture gaudy vases, or model fruit and flowers in wax. There may be some doubt as to the propriety of such employments in a farmer's daughter, but there can be none as to their uselessness in a clergyman's wife."

Patiently Miss Lætitia continued to bring forward one by one, the most promising of the serious young ladies in the neighbourhood, with whom her brother might have a chance of succeeding, for she knew very well that they all had been setting their caps at him ever since he had entered the parish, but the entire unprofitableness of their attentions somewhat astonished her. To every one an insurmountable objection was raised as soon as her name was mentioned.

Their regular attendance at private and public devotions, their zealous assistance at the schools and tea-meetings, their unexceptionable deportment and excessive amiability, had made no impression whatever. Scripture readers in their teens, and the most charming of tract distributors—fascinating widows, who held prayer-meetings once a week—and blooming matrons, indefatigable in making baby-linen and mutton-broth, were rejected with a want of appreciation that surprised her very much indeed.

"You must be difficult to please, Septimus," she observed, at last.

"Would you really then recommend any of these to me, Lætitia?"

She hesitated. In her affectionate heart, she thought none of them worthy of him, moreover she was not in a hurry for him to make his choice. Yet she remembered that the Bishop had held out a hope of advancement in his profession, if her brother profited by his kindly suggestion, and she was so devoted to his interest that she could not bring herself to hint at the undesirable change in her way of life it must inevitably bring to her.

"I think, Septimus, you should try to

please the Bishop and Lady Dorothea," she said at last; "it would no doubt be much to your advantage. You should go more into company, and increase as much as you can, the number of your female acquaintances. You have received an invitation to the Palace, why not go there? Lady Dorothea has a large circle of female friends."

The Curate did not appear to fancy the Bishop's wife as a medium in so delicate a matter, and rapidly recalled the figures and faces of the coterie, or rather petti-coaterie in which her ladyship flourished. But he saw nothing on which his heart could anchor.

He seemed to return to his paper, but instead of digesting the abuse of Anglicus & Co., he had surrendered his thoughts to an exceedingly pleasant reverie.

"O Lætitia, I must go my round," he cried, throwing down the newspaper, and starting suddenly to his feet.

His sister looked at him gravely as he buttoned up his coat, with a very thoughtful look, watched him take his hat and stick, and walk down the garden in the direction of the village. She took out her pocket-handkerchief, for a tear had fallen on either cheek.

Miss Mauleverer was sitting in her old panelled room, in her old home, in the carved oak-chair, placed as of yore close to the window which looked out upon those picturesque details that were comprised in a view of Middlecombe Regis from the Grange. She was partly engaged in admiring the important additions to the prospect that had sprung up since she had quitted the village, and partly occupied in thinking over other changes which had taken place in the neighbourhood within that period.

She had received a full account of the local news from her two faithful old servants, who partly from the pleasure of having their young mistress with them again, and partly from the satisfaction they received in dwelling on such subjects, were more than usually copious in their communications, especially with reference to the remarkable proceedings, life, character, and behaviour of that, to them, inexplicable, but rather agreeable personage, Lord Vallance.

But all her interest in these surprising narratives had subsided, and the novelty of her new position had vanished with it. She may have had the comfort of believing herself free of the entanglements her imprudence had brought upon her, but she knew that she was alone. Satisfactory explanations having been given, the marriage of Lord Lionel Leigh and Henrietta Drelincourt had taken place, and the happy pair had departed on their bridal tour up the Rhine.

Mr. Drelincourt had gone to London, to commence his parliamentary duties and mingle more in good society; the Marquis Mount-Trevor was in the Alps, renewing his acquaintance with guides, alpenstocks, crevasses, and glaciers; the Marchioness was at Geneva, where Lady Augusta was diligently pursuing a course of study under the most able teachers, with such steadiness as to promise more than the usual accomplishments.

Miss Stickles, too, had left Mount-Trevor Court; her new position of a married woman, with a husband of more than doubtful character, not quite "convening" with her post as governess to a young lady of title; and after many vain efforts to obtain tidings of the fugitive's whereabouts, she had returned to America.

No one in the neighbourhood had called upon the tenant of the Grange since her return. Mr. Ferdinand Stoughton, as I have said, had returned to his chambers in the Temple, therefore it was not in his power to show her any attention; but her more immediate neighbours, as she had ascertained, had not left their home, and she could not account for their neglect.

The fact is, Lady Vallance had been so freely talked about during her absence, that the people who had had any previous knowledge of Miss Mauleverer found a difficulty in making up their minds to a renewal of acquaintance. In particular, the serious young ladies who had formerly met her at schools or at tea-parties, affected to look half a dozen shades more serious when her name was mentioned in their presence.

Her uncle had gone back to his vineyard, Mr. Prodd having received instructions to telegraph to him when any reliable intelligence could be obtained of Lord Vallance;

and his friend the fashionable Catholic priest, who had been so zealous in her service, was, she knew, in London, engaged in organizing a new religious brotherhood, of which he had been appointed head. She seemed therefore totally without a friend.

While gazing on that bright addition to the landscape,—the group of new buildings designed by that eminent architect Mr. Vitruvius Palladio Crockett, F.S.A.,—her thoughts naturally reverted to the pure-minded and earnest clergyman, whose influence with the Lord of the Manor—founded on a sense of his worth as a parish priest—had caused their erection. She remembered his kindness to her, when she stood most in need of it, and how completely she had misunderstood its nature; and then she dwelt on his many amiable qualities, and the high character he had made for himself in the parish. She raised a comparison in her mind between him and her other clerical acquaintance, the Reverend Emanuel Mordecate. Mr. Fairholme she acknowledged was certainly not so handsome, nor could she think him so brilliant as his Roman Catholic brother; but then she knew him to possess sterling though homely qualities, of which she had seen no signs in the more fashionable preacher. The latter surprised his numerous admirers by his talents, the former rendered himself endeared to all who knew him, by his disinterestedness and sincerity.

Miss Mauleverer, in a pensive attitude, was absorbed in these pleasing recollections, when the door opened, and the object of her thoughts presented himself before her. She sprang up with an exclamation of pleasure and a smile of welcome, as she advanced holding out both hands. She had really felt a heavy depression on her spirits from his not having called upon her, and the gratification his unexpected appearance created appeared to him to render her features a thousand times more lovely than they had ever been before.

They may have lost something of the Carlo Dolce sweetness and of the Fra Angelico tenderness, that had once made so strong an impression on his mind. She was certainly not the Mater Dolorosa she in her first deep sorrow had appeared when he gazed down upon her from the pulpit of the old church on that memorable day. The spiritual pre-Raphaelite feeling had departed, but it had made way for something he found infinitely more admirable than any face the most famous illuminator had ever delineated.

As he now looked into her lustrous eyes, and regarded the smile and blush that brightened while they enriched her complexion, he could not help confessing that there was a spirit in the glance which met his, that no art however inspired could have transferred to canvas. It seemed to him not so much divinity humanized, as humanity eloquent with Divine attributes.

He shook hands with her, and led her back to her seat, expressing his pleasure at seeing her so much improved, in his usual quiet, friendly, undemonstrative way ; then sat down by her side apparently to talk over the affairs of his parish exactly in the old way. He did not seem at all embarrassed. His first glance on entering was certainly full of genuine admiration, but after that long look into her animated face, he regained his ordinary clerical indifference. The young lady, however, was not so soon restored to her wonted composure.

Mr. Fairholme at once began to talk of his new church, and finding an attentive listener, dwelt on its architectural beauties with more than *dilettant* enthusiasm. His companion evidently appreciated the description, and made remarks from time to time that proved to him that she had a far superior knowledge of the subject than the serious young ladies who had ventured to pour out upon him their gushing expressions.

He then dilated on the schools with equal eloquence, and was listened to with equal interest. It was very gratifying to him to hear the sensible observations on the education of the poor that broke in occasionally, but quite unobtrusively, upon the pauses of his description. They contrasted most favourably with the cut and dry aphorisms which the serious young ladies would volunteer, when he was only desirous that they should hold their tongues.

Lastly he dwelt on the comforts of his new dwelling, and the material advantages he possessed in having been blest with a home, in every way so worthy of a Christian minister. And again the comments of his companion were singularly in harmony with his own views of the dignity as well as responsibility of a parish priest—very different from the vapid commonplaces he had been in the habit of hearing from certain exceedingly attentive members of his congregation of the same sex.

"You may perhaps remember, Miss Mauleverer," continued the zealous Curate, "that I once had an idea."

"O yes!" replied his fair companion, laughing archly.

"It is not a sisterhood that I now think of establishing, though I have not entirely abandoned that intention. Every provision has been made in the parsonage for my comfort, but there seems to be one glaring deficiency, and I again come to you with the hope of profiting by your assistance."

"What is it you want, Mr. Fairholme?"

"A wife, Miss Mauleverer."

The young lady was again taken by surprise. She could not help divining the purport of this errand, and felt a sense of embarrassment she had never experienced before—no, not even in her first intercourse with Lord Lionel.

She could easily dispose of his former application, for she felt no disposition for the life of a recluse, but this present one was very different, and she could not dismiss it—a confused sense of her own loneliness, and of the nobleness of character of that truly good man who waited her reply, took from her all power of speech. At last she placed her hand in his, and looked the consent she found it impossible to express in words.

Mr. Fairholme was quite satisfied. He did not break out into any lover-like transports; he could not be so demonstrative even under such provocation, but expressed his gratitude briefly but fervently, and his conviction that much happiness was in store for them both.

CHAPTER XVI.

"LAST SCENE OF ALL."

A FEW months had elapsed since the event chronicled in the last chapter, and important changes had taken place. The zealous Curate of Middlecombe-Regis had become a married man, and the fair tenant of the Grange had been transformed into a clergyman's wife.

This had brought about a still more singular metamorphosis. Miss Lætitia had calmly surrendered her government of her brother's house to its new mistress, but had taken upon herself a rule of a still more onerous character. She became Lady Superior of a Protestant Sisterhood that had been established in the immediate neighbourhood in connection with an Orphanage; and never had so responsible an office been more worthily filled.

The Superior set an example to all the Sisters, not only in her devotions, but in her untiring zeal in benefiting those who required her good offices. She rigidly eschewed everything resembling luxurious indulgence, prayed like the rest, and fared in every way exactly as they did. She made no parade of her superiority, though she governed with an earnestness of purpose that exacted implicit obedience. In short the experiment was so judiciously carried out by her, that the amiable Bishop of Blankshire, with the full consent of Lady Theodosia, of course, accepted the office of visitor of the Sisterhood.

Among the sisters were noticed two energetic little women, who soon became known far and wide as Sister Dorcas, and Sister Charity; they were of course the reader's old acquaintances from the Grange, who had been partly persuaded by the Curate's sister to join her in the establishment, and partly been induced to comply by the necessity of finding another home,—the old building which had so long been their habitation, having been pulled down to make a site for the conventual structure that had been designed by the eminent London architect.

Lady Lionel Leigh was in London with her husband, waiting her presentation at Court, and the usual gaieties of a first regular season in town among good society. She enjoyed the happiness of living under the same roof as her father, simply because that excellent man had taken Lord Mount-Trevor's mansion in Belgrave Square, at a handsome rent, which was exceedingly convenient to the Marquis, as it enabled him to continue his mountain climbing, till he met with a rather bad fall on the ice, that deterred his lordship from attempting any further ascents. The fact is the Marquis was beginning to be aware that he was not quite so young as he had been, and in consequence made up his mind to leave off all athletic exercises.

The Marchioness was now with him at Nice, with the intention of remaining for the rest of the year in Italy, returning to England probably in the following London season, with her daughter. Lady Augusta's education had made such rapid progress that Lady Mount-Trevor thought of bringing her out next year, or at the furthest the year after—which ceremonial was expedited, I may as well here inform my readers, by a proposal of marriage from Sir Charles Forrester, in pursuance of an arrangement entered into between the playmates, when one was eight years old and the other fourteen.

Miss Lucretia Jefferson Stickles had returned safely to the States, where she had suddenly acquired considerable notoriety by turning orator. Female eloquence at political demonstrations in the North, was a novelty, and as the new speaker was very savage as well as intensely patriotic, she obtained immense applause and a good many dollars. The newspapers reported her orations at full length, and nothing was more fiery than her advocacy of Southern destruction, except her appeals for British extermination.

The only reliable intelligence that was ever obtained of Lord Vallance was written to Mrs.

Fairholme, and dated from Cariboo in British Columbia, acknowledging his Americian marriage, excusing his early abandonment of his bride, on the plea of having discovered that he had been quite as much deceived respecting her fortune, as he had been respecting her temper, which he solemnly assured his correspondent "no fellow could endure." He apologized for having contracted a second marriage under the circumstances, partly on account of the extenuating circumstances of the desirableness of such a union to him, and partly because he thought he had a right to consider himself a widower, not having heard of the existence of his wife for fifteen years.

He ended his communication by intimating that he had considered it necessary to change his name, not because his was plebeian, but for the opposite reason. In the first place it was too aristocratic for a digger—in the next he had never any legal right to it. The title was an Irish one, belonging to a kinsman who lived so retired a life in an obscure region of Connemara, that no one except a few near relatives knew of his existence.

Probably the reader may feel slightly interested in the fate of the three unworthies, whose several adventurous careers were so suddenly stopped in the small hours of a certain morning well remembered at Mount-Trevor Court. He may perhaps be glad to hear that, for a considerable period, they were doing quite as well as could be expected, in a safe marine residence provided for their accommodation in the Island of Portland. Indeed its estimable chaplain had given most hopeful reports of their individual cases.

The decayed tradesman was a regular attendant at chapel, and altogether most simple-minded and thoroughly inoffensive; the wax-flower manufacturer was an ingenious young man, with a remarkable capacity for intelligence, and singularly fond of tracts; and "the Downey One" a harmless simpleton, who was hardly responsible for his own actions—his sense of right and wrong being more confused than that of a child of six years old.

The warders would have given a very different estimate of the characters of these particular convicts, who, it was plain enough to their criminal experience, were working for an abbreviation of their term of imprisonment, and for tickets of leave. This indulgence it is probable they would have received in the usual course of prison maladministration, had not a hope of immediate escape induced them to join in a combined attack on their gaolers, when the inoffensive tradesman knocked the brains out of one of them; the ingenious young man, so fond of tracts, nearly throttled another to death, while shouting the most horrible blasphemies; and the harmless simpleton was within an ace of outwitting the entire establishment, and setting fire to the building in the confusion occasioned by the revolt.

There was a little miscalculation in the plot —a body of soldiers made their appearance on the Island long before they were expected, and a volley from their rifles put an end to the triumph of the too sanguine miscreants. The convicts Bunce and Chaffers were killed, and Smith was drowned while endeavouring to escape by plunging into the sea.

But of all the singular changes that had taken place, the most remarkable had occurred in the bye-street in Belgravia. Mrs. Bootles had left off letting furnished apartments. When she lost her three guineas a-week, as well as her terrible anxieties respecting her mysterious lodger, the manager's widow appeared to have contracted a distaste for secular matters altogether. She went more frequently to chapel, but not to the one she had previously attended.

Miss Bootles gave up the Honorary Secretaryship of the Ragged School, and retired into private life. Finally Mrs. Bootles gave up the house. Neither was ever heard of again in Belgravia, and it was only by accident the discovery was made some months afterwards that they had gone over to the Church of Rome, and had immured themselves for life in a Belgian convent.

No. 9 had also a bill in the window, announcing that it was to be let or sold. Yes, that "*bijou* of a furnished house" was empty—its tenant, who had so frequently scandalized her opposite neighbours, and disturbed the peace as well as the propriety of the street, having concluded her tenancy. One morning all that remained of the once attractive driver of the pretty ponies, and the smart carriage, was taken away from her almost deserted habitation by a vehicle of a totally different character. A one-horsed hearse carried her to the cemetery, a gaunt, superannuated char-woman being the only mourner in attendance.

At the "Queen's Head" round the corner, her entire history was thoroughly ventilated, and it became known that she had been the daughter of a disreputable dog-fancier, who used to hang about low public-houses in Westminster, leaving a ragged wife and half-naked daughter to starve in a back room in a filthy court, or wander about the streets picking up what they could.

As the latter grew up she attracted the attention of a sporting horse-dealer, and was easily induced to quit a miserable home, rendered intolerable by the frequent quarrels of the drunken dog-fancier and his half-starved wife. She quickly learnt riding and driving, and as she was enabled to dress well, her youthful figure and pretty face attracted the attention of admirers holding a high social position. The horse-dealer was discarded, the *bijou* of a furnished house in the bye-street in Belgravia accepted her as its mistress, and, in the neatest little turn-out in town, she quickly drove her way into being the fashion to look at, to talk about, and, with a certain class, to visit.

But the vices she had imbibed in her early training could not be concealed, and soon gained force, the means of indulgence being always available. Intemperate habits quickly developed a consumptive tendency; and having, by her violence, driven away from her all her fashionable friends, she rapidly sunk. The one-horsed hearse and the solitary mourner proclaimed the end. A benevolent Catholic priest in the neighbourhood, who had been called in at the last extremity, had, after considerable trouble, discovered the latter in the union workhouse, she being the only survivor of the dying Magdalen's abandoned home.

Of this reverend gentleman I have more to say, another of the houses in the same street being in his occupation. This was the building the alterations in which had so strongly excited the curiosity of the Honorary Secretary to the Ragged School. It in due time became a Roman Catholic religious institution, with the title of "The Brotherhood of the Sacred Heart."

The establishment, of course, consisted entirely of men, their principal habit being closely-buttoned coats of dark cloth, that reached down to their heels. They appeared to be almost all young men of very pale complexions and of very grave aspect, who occupied themselves in teaching, praying, fasting, visiting the sick, and relieving the poor. Among them were the scions of several Protestant families, chiefly zealous young clergymen, who fancied that they were called to adopt a monastic life. Of the converts the most distinguished was Lord Clarence Leigh.

It was not at all surprising that this young man should have entered the Brotherhood, for the Father Superior was his tutor, by whose arguments his conversion had been effected. His ecclesiastical superiors, as a singular proof of their confidence and regard, had appointed the Reverend Emanuel Mordecate the head of a newly organized religious body, composed almost entirely of persons he had been the means of bringing over from the heresy of Luther to the only true and apostolic church, and had caused it to be established in the fashionable district in which his zealous exertions had accomplished so many important triumphs.

The Father Superior was alone in the chamber that had been set apart for his private use. It was something better in its appearance than those of "the Brotherhood," which had been made to look as much like monkish cells as possible—the bare walls having no ornament except a crucifix; the room no other furniture than a pallet of the coarsest kind. The apartment of the Father Superior was a sitting-room. It contained shelves filled with devotional books, an engraving of Pope Pius IX. in a black frame, and another of the Madonna and Child; also a writing-table and two or three chairs, a *prie-dieu*, and an altar surmounted by a representation of Calvary; but to modern ideas of comfort it looked singularly bare and uninviting.

The Reverend Emanuel Mordecate had retired here for his private devotions—the public service for that portion of the day he having just superintended in the chapel of the building—the parlours, very much changed in appearance, being so called. On entering he had on a strange-looking hat, projecting very much in front and behind. He did not take it off. He closed the door and stood still, when a change became visible in that calm spiritual physiognomy that had made him regarded by his female admirers as so wonderfully like a saint.

He sunk on his knees as this change of expression was becoming more manifest, and with hands clasped and eyes raised towards a certain portion of the sky seen from the window, he murmured his prayers. Again they were not in the language or ritual prescribed by either the Protestant or Romish Churches. They were in a totally different tongue. They were neither in English nor Latin—every word was Hebrew. And as they were repeated, a child-like innocency of feeling seemed to obliterate the subtlety and guile which had been impressed upon the human mask of the Jesuit.

Presently he rose, took off his hat, and flung himself into the *prie-dieu*, throwing himself back, gazing upon vacancy, and surrendering his mind to the day-dreams that are so often the recreation of the enthusiast and the adventurer. But they did not carry him to the grandeur of the Vatican; they were not made brilliant with any of the glories of Romish ambition. They brought to his mind the same humble interior they had always brought—the quiet little bed-room over the curiosity shop in the Kalver-Straat at Amsterdam; and they set before him the same touching domestic picture with which his heart had been moved a thousand times.

The sweet face of his mother, the exquisitely tender voice of the beautiful Jewess, teaching him the faith his fathers had received direct from Jehovah, who had divided the great waters and brought His chosen people safely out of the land of bondage. And he covered the human mask with his hands and wept. Wept with the contrition of a man mastering the emotion of a child; wept passionately, convulsively, like one surrendering his nature to an impulse that must be obeyed.

While thus absorbed in the indulgence of feelings that ought to have been foreign to his ostensible nature, for they led him very far from his assumed position, footsteps were heard ascending, and presently there was a knocking at his door. He had scarcely time to remove the traces of severe mental suffering from his face when, at his permission to enter, the door opened, and the hollow face and lack lustre eyes of the most ascetic of the Brotherhood, became visible.

"A visitor to the Reverend Father Superior!" drawled a nasal voice.

The announcement was followed by a short stout man, very shabbily dressed, in a loose old brown coat, tied round the waist by a coarse shawl, that did not fit him in the least, and a loose pair of well worn trousers, the ends of which were tucked into a very large and loose pair of boots that had evidently seen quite 'as much service. His face was more remarkable than his person. His massive head was covered with a dirty red and white turban, from which heavy locks of very black hair escaped. Strongly marked features, of an exceedingly dark complexion, were almost hidden under a long black beard, but that could not conceal a prominent nose and unusually large brilliant black eyes.

The man was unquestionably a foreigner,—it was equally clear that he was a Jew. If there was an individual of any nation that the celebrated Catholic preacher was indifferent about, it was one of the children of Israel. No doubt, he could have tolerated a Rothschild or a Montefiore, but it so happened that they had carefully avoided his society; but, from some cause or other, a low Jew was his special abomination. His feelings therefore may be imagined when, almost as soon as the door had closed behind him, and the ascetic brother had begun to descend the stairs, the stranger threw his arms round the Father Superior, and embraced him with the most lively demonstrations of affection.

"Mine tear poy! mine tear poy!" he exclaimed, in broken English, his bright eyes flashing, and his dark countenance glowing with unusual excitement.

"May I ask, sir, the meaning of this?" cried the Father Superior, indignantly, making ineffectual attempts to free himself; for he was not without apprehensions that such demonstrations, from such a visitor, if observed, might produce mischievous consequences.

"O my tear poy! I am Lazarus Cohen, your tear mother's only prother."

There was another hug, but the recipient took it more patiently than the first. Cohen he knew was his mother's maiden name, and he remembered also that she had often talked to him of a brother from whom she had long been parted.

"Ah, my tearest sister Esther!" the man cried, passionately. "I have cause to cherish her memory, for she to me was as the rose of Sharon in the wilderness and as a fountain of sweet waters in the desert."

The priest smoothed his ruffled features, and permitted his white hand to be held in the brown palm of his kinsman. He seemed to hear a strain of familiar music.

"Listen, my tear poy. When I was ruined by that Dutch thief of a burgomaster, Vander Scamppe by taking his collection of vamily pictures at half what he valued them at, and sending them for sale to Paris, the Gerard Dows, the Ostades, the Cuyps, the Rembrandts, the Hobbimas, the Albert Durers, the Teniers, the Ruysdaels, turned out to be copies, and they were sold for almost noting.

I was without a stiver and could obtain no redress, for Vander Scamppe made a joke of how he had done a Jew, and our peoples were angry with me for my folly. Then your tearest mother, my sister Esther, come to me with a bag of ducats that she had saved, and placing it in my hands told me it was all she had, but it might do for me to begin the world again, if I was prudent; and advised me to travel in the East, and deal in jewels, in which way certain of our peoples had made much monies.

"So my tear poy I went to India, with my bag of ducats, which I presently turn into gold mohurs. I travel about from one country to another and I change my mohurs for diamonds and emeralds and rubiės, which I sell again to Rajahs and Ranees for more mohurs. And then I buy again jewelled sabres and bangles and armour and shawls, and I journey from Calcutta to Bokhara, buying and selling, sometimes with Indian princes, sometimes with English officers, and make much profit everywhere.

"Presently come mutiny and I am at Delhi, and first from the richer rebels who want money to escape, and next from the soldiers who plunder their palaces, I get enormous treasure of all kinds, for my mohurs, or sovereigns, of which I have an equal store. Then I go to my Lord Canning and sell him shawls, arms, jewels, everyting rich and curious he desire to have, and am richest Jew in India.

"All this time I think much of my tearest sister Esther whose bag of ducats I have turn to such great profits; but I hear only that she marry Emanuel Mordecai, of the Kalver-Straat who has died of fever leaving her a widow with one son; and at last I pack up my jewels and my other Indian treasures and take ship for Amsterdam.

"I arrive safe, and am welcomed by my peoples, who have hear of me as the wealthiest diamond merchant in the world. I go to reward my tearest sister Esther for the bag of ducats she had saved. But woe to my heart, she was taking her long rest in the cemetery of our peoples, and the house in the Kalver-Straat was empty, and shut up. I ask our peoples for her son, but they shake their heads and spit on the ground, and I learn that he went to England to the care of a kinsman who had turned Christian.

"I buy the house in the Kalver-Straat because it was her house. I take ship for England in search of my lost kinsman, because you were her son. I have sold much precious stones at large profits, and made much inquiry of our peoples here about the son of my tearest sister, Esther, but they only shake their heads, and spit on the ground.

"The God of my fathers has been good to me, as He was to our father Abraham and to father Isaac and to father Jacob. He gave me tidings of you, after much journeyings to and fro, blessed be His holy name! I followed traces of you from place to place, and I have found you at last.

"But my tear poy!" he added, looking scrutinizingly round the room, and then searchingly into the Father Superior's face; "*Dosh it pay?*"

The Father Superior affected not to understand the question, but there was an expression on his face which he could not conceal.

"If I had found you a Poᴜe, or a Cardinal,

or even a Bishop, I should say my nephew Emanuel knows what he is about. But it is plain to me that this sort of thing dosh not pay. The Christians have took you in, my tear poy, as that thief of Vander Scamppe deceived me about his vamily pictures. It is a discredit to our peoples to allow themselves to be took in, and I can feel for you, for I know what it is.

"Look here, my tear poy!" He went cautiously to the door, opened it, and looked out, then closed it softly and returned to the Father Superior, drawing a morocco case from an inner pocket. The old man came close to his side, and opened the case, his brilliant black orbs twinkling with a peculiar satisfaction as he watched the passive face of his kinsman.

In a moment there flashed upon the priest's eyes a lustre that involuntarily made them blink, and a cry of admiration escaped his lips. Resting on cushions of dark velvet, lay several diamonds, rubies, and emeralds of extraordinary size and beauty — the first apparently unrivalled in weight, cutting, and purity.

"What do you tink of dem, my tear Emanuel?"

"They are very beautiful," replied the Father Superior.

The old Jew chuckled, and stroked his long beard.

"Peautiful, aha! I should tink so, my tear poy!"

He took up a magnificent diamond, and made its light flash from the darkness, then whispered, "That was from the imperial crown of the Great Mogul."

Having placed it back carefully, he took up a ruby, with which he played in like manner.

"Here is de eye of de most famous idol in all Hindostan. The goot priest sell it me, and put cut-glass in its place; which do just as well for every pody—and mosh better for me."

He raised an emerald, "This was in an amulet worn by a Maharajah, which I puy of an Irish drummer for a bottle of whisky, a silver watch, a clasp knife of many blades, a relic in a crucifix, and five sovereigns. Your Mister Hope, he shall want to puy it of me for twenty tousand pounds."

The Father Confessor looked astonished.

"Dis case," said Lazarus Cohen, in another whisper, "is worth a quarter of a million sterling. And I have rough stones and cut stones, of more dan twice as much value, peside gold ornaments, and oriental fabrics of most precious kind, dat shall make me worth altogether more dan a million English monies. A goot return for de bag of ducats your tearest mother give to me of her savings, because I was a ruined man."

The Father Superior looked and felt interested.

The old Jew put back the case into the pocket of an inner vest, and brought out another from a place of equal security. His kinsman expected to see more precious stones. He started with an exclamation of surprise. He was shown the miniature of a singularly handsome woman. He gazed on the beautiful features with a sense of ecstacy impossible to be described, for he recognized the face which in his day-dreams had illumined so lovingly the well-remembered chamber over the curiosity-shop in the Kalver-Straat, at Amsterdam.

The black orbs were twinkling very pleasantly as they noticed his emotion. The Father Superior, too much moved to speak, turned an appealing look to his companion.

"Dat is my taughter, Esther," the old man murmured into his ear, greedily watching the expression of his face—a mask no longer.

"I marry among my peoples that I find rich bankers in India. I have one child. I name her after your tearest mother, who gave me her savings when I am a poor, broken-down, ruined Jew."

Lazarus Cohen came closer to his kinsman, and whispered into his ear, with his black eyes more lustrous than ever, as they maintained their watch upon the priest's face.

"I have taken so much troubles in search of de only son of my tearest sister, to say to him, out of my love for your tearest mother, I offer you my daughter in marriage—with half my fortune at once, and the rest when I go to join my father Abraham. What you say, my tear Emanuel?"

The Father Superior, with a mighty effort, seemed to take his fascinated gaze from the lovely countenance, so attractively displayed on the ivory, covered his agitated face with his hands, and sank back helplessly on the nearest seat.

"No, no!" he cried passionately. "It cannot be. It is a thing totally impossible."

"But dese Christians have took you in, my tear poy!" exclaimed the Jew, with mingled indignation and pity. "I am shure it dosh not pay. If you was a Pope, or a Cardinal, or a Bishop, I should not complain. But dis place is not goot enough for you at all, and you shall come and live wid me in de home of your tearest mother in the Kalver-Straat. What do you tink of that, my tear Emanuel?"

"I cannot think of it!" exclaimed the Father Superior, in increased excitement. "I am shut out from the slightest approach to anything of the kind."

"You must have time for consideration," whispered the Jew. "Remember you vosh took in. Remember it dosh not pay. Remember my daughter Esther is the image of your tearest mother, and that you shall be de happiest as well as de richest Jew in Holland; and when you have remembered everyting in a sensible way, like one of our peoples, write to me at Moses Bendixen's, in the Crutched Friars. Adieu, my tear poy."

The Father Confessor shook hands with his kinsman, and accompanied him to the street-door—the old man looking narrowly at the signs of poverty and privation that the new institution presented. At the door the latter again cordially shook hands, as he stooped his bearded brown face close to the priest's ear.

"It dosh not pay—you vosh took in," he whispered, and then made his way out of the bye-street towards the neighbouring square, his dark eyes glistening like his diamonds, as he played with his curly black beard, evidently content with his mission.

Nevertheless the Father Superior returned to his religious duties as if no temptation of any kind had been offered him; as if he had never heard of the diamond merchant, his daughter, and his wealth; as if he had abandoned all thought of the dear home in the Kalver-Straat at Amsterdam. His sermons at the chapel were more fashionably attended, and seemed to gain in force as well as in popularity. Moreover, he was making advance in the confidence of his ecclesiastical superiors.

Suddenly it became known that he was

going on a secret mission of the greatest importance, to Rome. It was said to be one of vast consequence to the only true and Apostolic Church. The mystery with which it was enveloped excited an unusual amount of speculation. Indeed, many zealous Catholics confidently asserted that it was nothing less than a proposal from the Anglican prelates to the Holy Father, which was to lead to the admission of the entire Protestant Establishment into the system of the Papacy.

The Father Superior took leave of the Brotherhood in a very moving address, as well as of all friends in Belgravia, in a sermon that was equally affecting. Moreover, he wrote to his friend Monsignor, with the most earnest eloquence, expressing the joy he should feel in once more enjoying the priceless blessing of returning to the capital of the Christian world.

The Father Superior left London on the day appointed for his departure, but he never reached Rome, and was never again seen by "the Brethren of the Sacred Heart," by his fashionable congregation, or by any of his English friends.

THE END.

CPSIA information can be obtained
at www.ICGtesting.com
Printed in the USA
LVHW040340110522
718423LV00001B/281

9 783375 007003